Harry Furniss

Pen and Pencil in Parliament

Harry Furniss

Pen and Pencil in Parliament

ISBN/EAN: 9783337106539

Printed in Europe, USA, Canada, Australia, Japan

Cover: Foto ©Andreas Hilbeck / pixelio.de

More available books at **www.hansebooks.com**

PEN AND PENCIL

IN

PARLIAMENT

COMPILED AND ILLUSTRATED

BY

HARRY FURNISS

LONDON

SAMPSON LOW, MARSTON & COMPANY
(LIMITED)
St. Dunstan's House
FETTER LANE, FLEET STREET, E.C.

1897

PRINTED BY
SPOTTISWOODE & CO., NEW-STREET SQUARE
LONDON

PREFACE

I MUST confess that I approached my task of compiling this volume with some anxiety. It is true that I have enjoyed exceptional opportunities, not only as Parliamentary artist to Mr. 'Punch' for many years, but also in studying men and manners in Parliament for other periodicals. It is true that the views of the House with which I illustrate my random remarks are the crystallised impressions produced by years of careful observation in all parts of the House—that House I know and love so well—where, I may say, the sound of the division bell is as sweet music to my ears, and the light from the clock-tower a beacon which guides me to my second home. Nevertheless, I feel the utmost diffidence in placing this volume before the public. The truth is, my subject is rather a heavy one to handle. The Parliamentary pie is not easily digested. The ingredients are anything but light, and the plums are few. And, although the very dulness of St. Stephen's has been its chief fascination for me—I suppose much in the same way that a burlesque always saddens me, while a tragedy invariably makes me laugh—yet I can hardly expect that my readers will view the matter quite in the same way. For my own part I can only plead that I have done my best to lighten it as much as possible, and to provide sufficient sauce to render the dish acceptable to all. That is so far as a caricaturist is allowed to go. Not that the age in which we live does not offer scope for the genius of a Hogarth, a Rowlandson, or a Gillray, were they alive, but because my subject is chaste and respectable, and because nowadays the

wings of the caricaturist have been clipped, and he is no longer allowed to
soar to the heights which the old masters of the art scaled so effectively.
Instead of yielding to his fancies and sharpening his claws against the
vices and impostures of the age, the caricaturist of to-day must content
himself with its follies and frivolities.   He is judged now by his skill in
hitting off the fold of a coat or the turn of a collar.   The clothes, in fact,
rather than the man, must be his theme, and nobody cares how cleverly he
portrays the cant or cowardice of the wearer.   And yet there has been no
period to compare with the last twelve or fifteen years for freedom of speech,
and for freedom of pen in dealing with political matters.   Now that Home
Rule is dead, and the lion has lain down with the lamb, one forgets the
extent of personal attack, of virulent abuse, of the gross personalities, of
savage acrimony introduced into every section of our political life, both
inside and outside of the House of Commons.   There never was a time
in which the Press—including even our magazines—was fuller of criticisms
of public men ; there never was a time when the Pulpit was used more as
a medium for public denunciation of public men than it has been during
this same period.   Yet, at the same time, the one man who by nature is
intended to be a critic—I mean the caricaturist—is coerced into effeteness.

Why is it that in the field of political criticism rival politicians throw
mud at each other, and the next day when they meet shake hands ?   Why
is it that the political writer flings ink at his opponent, and the next day
hobnobs with him ?   Say what you like, preach what you like, write what you
like, the friend you criticise shrugs his shoulders, smiles, and shakes hands.
But caricature that man, however deservedly, even though indulgently, you
run the risk of making him your enemy for life.   Not your really big man, for
he is above such things.   It is your second- or third-raters, your little men,
who would be big had they the ability, who, when you, as a caricaturist,
honour them with notice, spit at you in return for the implied compliment.

But there is a worse enemy to the caricaturist: it is the man who is looking on and poisons the mind of the good-natured subject of caricature against the caricaturist. My long experience has been to discover that, if any bad feeling has been raised between myself and my subjects – subjects worthy of notice—it has not been that my subject has taken offence at seeing anything in my caricatures that was not intended in good part, but that 'damned good-natured friends' have been at work to point out a motive that never was entertained.

Among the drawings in this little work, which presents a fraction of my political caricatures, with few exceptions designed since my withdrawal from an old friend under whose wing I published the greater portion of my work in that direction, but none of which, of course, appear in this volume, I am quite prepared to find that some will hardly be popular with those who take a different view from myself of the public men and public events with whom and with which they deal; although I maintain that the view I took when these drawings were made was the correct one, as shown by the present state of politics in our country. And I must ask my readers to recollect that these sketches were made at a time when political feeling ran high. There is very little excitement in politics now, and naturally, when going over republished sketches of events that have passed, one must remember that they are presented in the hope of their being historically interesting, and certainly 'without prejudice.'

HARRY FURNISS.

LONDON, 1897.

Before the opening of Parliament a search is regularly made in the cellars for any descendant of Guy Fawkes.
Query : What would happen if he were to be found ? Anything like this ?

 STEPHEN'S supplies endless material for pen and pencil. Every day upon which the House is sitting, columns of the newspapers are devoted to Parliamentary proceedings, whilst nine-tenths of the paragraphs in the more gossipy portions of the journals have their origin in the *on dits* of the Lobbies. Moreover, even the provincial papers, at great expense, have all matters of interest in Parliament telegraphed to them, but they are treated all too seriously.

There is a great deal that is grotesque in Parliament, from the searching for Guy Fawkes on the opening day, to the cry of the janitors of 'Who goes home ?' when the House rises at the end of each sitting. Poor Guy Fawkes would have little chance of hiding now in the basement of the Houses of Parliament. There is no drawing-room in the mansions of London so beautifully kept as that part of the building ; even a beetle, should one exist there, has no chance of crawling across the floor, for the place is well manned with attendants, and well watched by the police ;

A POLITICAL GUY FAWKES.
See page 5.

although, strange to say, the year before last, the whole House of Commons was roused to a high pitch of excitement in the middle of a most important subject by the appearance of a little mouse on the floor of the House itself, and the Serjeant-at-Arms was called forward to do his duty like a man.

The cry of 'Who goes home?' is also somewhat out of date, considering that it was originally to summon those Members going home to protect their

If the searchers are really anxious to be successful in their Guy-hunt they might very well exchange the cellars for the Woolsack, for, on the opening day, the Lord Chancellor and the four Royal Commissioners are compelled by tradition to make guys of themselves. These noble Lords will be easily recognised by those who have seen the 'Humours of Parliament.'

Speaker from highwaymen in his journey from Parliament to his house. The same custom prevailed in the theatres of those early days, that those going home should sort themselves, for protection's sake, into batches for the different districts. Seeing that the Speaker now goes into his apartments without leaving the building, and that most Members disappear from St. Stephen's after their work in hansoms or four-wheelers, the cry of 'Who goes home?' merely means 'All out.'

The picturesque figure of Guy Fawkes will always be a valuable one to the carica-

turist, the latest being Lord Rosebery, when he hinted that he wished to blow the House of Lords out of existence.

I trust those who write so exhaustively on the Parliament Houses begin at the beginning of the day's work, when those men dressed like French cooks are busily dusting the furniture; and that they do thorough justice to all the underground Parliament, to the kitchens, to the great improvement in respect of baths in the House, and other matters so important to the health of our legislators; also that they in some way explain why, in spite of the wonderful sanitary arrangements of the House, it still remains one of the most unhealthy places in London; that if there are any microbes about they seem to find their way into the Legislative Chamber of the House of Commons. This very year quite a number of Members are laid up at home with the 'grip,' dreaming of the influenzal House of Commons. Because if these gentlemen have not dwelt sufficiently on these important matters, I shall myself have to bring out

another book dealing exclusively with this part of the subject. Not treating, as I have treated, Sir William Harcourt as the cook of the House, or Lord Salisbury as the new broom, or Mr. Cremer making a clean sweep of the officials of the House, but really going into the matter seriously.

Perhaps there is no place in the world where man's comfort is so fully considered as in The Best Club in England, from the Speaker's throne to the private Member's arm-chair. And, before I give my random recollections of the men and their manners, I may be pardoned for touching briefly on the comforts provided for gentlemen in St. Stephen's.

'An Englishman's house is his castle,' and an Englishman's arm-chair is his throne. Not the gilded, stilted, uncomfortable erection of

THAW! MARCH, 1895.

which one sees an imitation at Madame Tussaud's, but the easy, well-padded, well-worn, common or sitting-room arm-chair.   How sacred is it held to the master of the

THE NEW BROOM.   JUNE, 1895.

house!   How jealous is its owner that no one else shall occupy it!   How careful his wife, olive-branches, and servants that the haven of rest for the head of the family shall remain untenanted and undisturbed, save by him.   Never was happiness known by the

man who possessed an uncomfortable arm-chair; never did there exist a shrewd wife
who allowed her lord and master to sit in one that was not a treasure of luxury.
Sitting at his feet what time he is installed comfortably in that easy chair, before a
cheerful fire, she can wheedle from him promises and favours that could not be
extorted by the terrors of the rack. It is not, therefore, to be wondered at that in
Clubland are provided easy chairs of the acme of Sybaritic luxury; were it otherwise,
the Members would be much more frequently found at home; while it goes without
saying that 'the best club in England—the House of Commons—is accommodated
with the most luxurious and comfortable of chairs, in greater variety than I have seen
anywhere else; in fact, there are, as I have remarked from the platform, 'high chairs,
low chairs, soft chairs, hard chairs, big chairs, little chairs, round chairs, square chairs,
wide chairs, narrow chairs, spring chairs, cane chairs, rocking chairs, chairs on wheels,
saddle-bag chairs, and last, but most curious, *straddle* chairs—chairs that equestrian
Members can mount when they have lost their morning canter in the Row, and fancy
themselves in pigskin.' The chairs, indeed, are made to fit all sorts and conditions
of M.P.s. This round-backed, squat-looking chair, for instance, looks built to receive
the portly form of a T. B. Potter, who would not trust himself upon the delicately
fashioned straddle chair, preferring to leave it to become the mount of the sport-loving
'Jemmy' Lowther; whilst the low rocking chair is most inviting to the languidly
disposed, say either of the Balfours—the æsthetic, long-legged Arthur James, the

MR. CREMER AND HIS SUCCESSFUL SWEEP. JUNE, 1895.

popular leader, and the equally lengthy and popular G. B. Balfour. No particular
chair, however, is appropriated by any one Member, but there are certain faddists,
some of whom object to sitting on leather, some have a rooted aversion to velvet,
and others display a preference for chintz ; but no one need grumble, for there are
chairs to satisfy Members with all kinds of predilections.

This variety is due to the fact that the providing of the furniture of the House is a matter
of selection, and is not done by contract with
any one firm, in which case there might be a
certain amount of sameness about it. Mishaps
and breakages, it is strange to say of such a large
assembly, are very rare, except, perhaps, in the
refreshment department.

A MOUSE! May, 1895.

There the forks are frequent victims, coming sadly to grief through being utilised
as impromptu corkscrews. When a Member, parched by impassioned oratory, or
vociferous party cheering, desires to form a closer acquaintance with the contents of his
hurriedly-ordered bottle, he scorns to wait for the orthodox cork-extractor of commerce,
but presses a fork into service instead, with results, as a rule, much more disastrous to

the fork than effective upon the cork, the exertions
made with the harmless, necessary prandial instrument causing it to assume shapes weird and bizarre
to look upon. These shapes vary in nature according to the temperaments of their respective manipu-
lators, and the appearance of the maltreated fork
after the operation ought to enlighten the least
observant mind as to the character of the impetuous
Member. One fork, for instance, has lost an
outside prong, but is otherwise uninjured. This is
a simple piece of circumstantial evidence. It requires no Sherlock Holmes to deduce from the
condition of that fork, by an elaborate system of

MR. POTTER TAKES HIS
BATH.

ratiocination, the nature of its wielder. He inserted that fork between cork and bottle,
applied a downward pressure, snap went his lever prong, and, guilty fear overcoming
his thirst and impatience, he refrained from further ill-treatment of his extempore corkscrew, and probably concealed the mutilated remains in his pocket, till such time as he
could dispose of them unobserved.

Determination and physical force are denoted by the appearance of the wreck of

THE INFLUENZIAL MEMBER DREAMS OF THE INFLUENZA IN THE HOUSE.

fork number two. The Member who used it evidently meant to get that cork out at all hazards. What recked he of the breaking off of his lever prong? Three still remained, but, before the welcome pop of the emerging cork greeted the thirsty Member's ears, yet another prong had been sacrificed on the altar of Bacchus.

A glance at the third improvised corkscrew is sufficient to reveal the perseverance of the politician by whom it was handled. One outside prong has succumbed to the strain of leverage, and, after it had been placed *hors de combat*, the Member turned his attention to its fellow on the other side. This one was obstinate and refused to snap, but the Member was obstinate also, and screwed away until he twisted the prong completely round, as evidenced by the kink in the middle. Whether success ultimately crowned his efforts I know not, but he deserved it.

Many of these mutilated, tell-tale implements, however, are not discovered, having been consigned by the peccant Members to a watery grave over the side of the Terrace Wall.

The Refreshment Department of to-day is very different from that of the days of Palmerston. Complete and well-appointed, it is qualified nowadays to cater for and pander to the tastes of an epicure; but in the time of 'Pam' and his colleagues the arrangements were very primitive, and the great statesman and his contemporaries had to content themselves with a baron of beef placed upon the table in the kitchen.

To revert, however, to the upholstery of the House itself, there is a certain kind of damage, or wear and tear, that is brought about in a rather curious manner. Some Members (one in particular, who shall be nameless) whilst sitting in the House are so nervous and agitated, that they keep up an involuntary movement with their feet, shifting them perpetually backwards and forwards until they eventually succeed in completely wearing out the material under them.

The seats of the two Houses provide, in the matter of colour, another item of difference between the Gilded Chamber of the Peers and that of their less exalted fellow-politicians, green being the predominating hue in the Commons, whilst the Peers recline upon scarlet, though in the old House of Lords the cushions were maroon. One of the unwritten laws in connection with the furniture of that august assembly is that, when the Sovereign opens Parliament, no Member of the House of Lords must lean back in his seat. To obviate the unwitting or, perchance, defiant committal of such a dire offence against the Majesty of the Throne, the seats of the Upper House are furnished with removable backs, which are let down in the presence of the Sovereign, so that the aristocratic politicians must of necessity preserve a posture upright and respectful. If these backs were constructed so as to drop suddenly and simultaneously on the touching of a button or the pressing of a knob, Royalty might be provided with some unrehearsed effects by the dignified Peers of the realm. For, were the Sovereign to put in an appearance at the Gilded Chamber unexpectedly, noble lords drowsing on the benches, and dreaming of a good run with the hounds across the slopes of Leicestershire, or a shooting battue on the Highland moors, would find themselves suddenly executing a back somersault, more befitting an acrobat on the stage of the variety theatre, than a blue-blooded politician in the sacred chamber of debate. What a delightfully ludicrous spectacle for the regal eyes, and how Bluff King Hal or either of the Cavalier Charleses would have enjoyed effecting a sudden entrance and witnessing the involuntary gymnastics of their austere lawmakers! The seats are not constructed so in the Commons, for the Sovereign never goes there.

THE Speakership of the House of Commons is the most distinguished position a Commoner can aspire to, and is in fact that of 'the First Commoner in England.' It is a great post, but it does not require a great man. Tact and very little else is necessary. For, as in playing the character of Hamlet, no actor has ever been known to fail, so in playing the part of the Speaker, it is, as actors say, a part that plays itself. The figure in Shakespeare's play, always in the centre of the stage, is safe for effect; dressed in solemn black, it gains when compared with the gorgeous habiliments of the King and the Queen, and the simplicity of Ophelia dressed in white. So is the Speaker in the chair in the House of Commons, with wig and gown, a contrast to the ordinary Member in his every-day attire. Still, tact entails a multitude of talents, and we must say that in our time the Speakers have all proved equal to the honour thrust upon them. There is no doubt that the Chairmanship of Committees is a far more difficult position, and one that has to be filled without pomp, without the advantage of the elevated position, without a wig and gown, and without thanks. It is when a Bill is in the Committee stage

THE CONY-BEAR AND THE SPEAKER.

that the Chairman has to be on his mettle, and better acquainted with the details of the measure than anyone else, except the Minister, or the Member who has charge of it. If he has not learned his lesson well, it leads to a great loss of time. Mr. Courtney was acknowledged an ideal Chairman of Committees, but the House would not hear of him as Speaker. He was too dictatorial; in fact, he was too clever. Dignity and tact he troubled very little about ; he was the schoolmaster, the professor, the lecturer ; and, although in Committee the House is probably somewhat like a school, or the debating society of a college, and requires to be lectured and scolded, and to feel that whoever presides knows a great deal more than anyone who is speaking ; still, it does not do for the

Chairman to show by his tone and gesture that he is a superior scholar to those under him.

In the time I touch upon, Speaker Brand had perhaps a far more difficult post than Speaker Peel, for it was in the former's time that obstruction was originated, was rampant, was legislated for and strangled. And when the latter took the chair he found the monster slain—at least, not quite slain, scotched, not killed. But still, although he had to go through as much as did his predecessor, he had a weapon for the obstructionists that Speaker Brand had not.

It is needless for me to touch upon the

THE SPEAKER'S BROTHER.

MISS PARLIAMENTINA SOLVES THE PROBLEM OF THE SPEAKERSHIP.

SIR WILLIAM (*as he 'peels' Campbell-Bannerman of the Speaker's robes*): '*If I am not to be Speaker, I'll take good care that Bannerman isn't.*'

behaviour of certain Members to the First Commoner, of the insults thrown at the Chair. But there is little doubt that no one holding an honourable and dignified office in any other position in the country is subjected to such rough treatment as is the Speaker of the House of Commons. In the excitement of political warfare, carried to such a pitch in the few years just past, when the Chair was simply attacked and its dignity abused with as little regard as any other assailable post or department, Members in their party fervour so far forgot themselves as to be—it is not too hard a word to use—inhuman. When the Chair as an institution representing the Sovereign was attacked, the Speaker, with that dignity so natural to him, soon put an end to such tactics ; but it has been noticed by many that when it paid the aggressive party to worry the Chair, means were adopted that simply amounted to torturing an English gentleman.

It is bad enough for the First Commoner in England to have to listen to tedious, pointless, unnecessary harangues, and no one can deny that Patience on a monument was never better personified than in the case of the Speaker of the House of Commons. No Speaker ever left the Chair more respected or admired than was the last. His rulings were characterised by great firmness and decision; he was invariably most attentive and courteous to all; indeed, I am using no extravagant terms of laudation when I say that, notwithstanding the illustrious names which adorn the long roll of his predecessors in the high position which he filled, it is universally conceded in the House that there never has been, and that there is never likely to be, a more popular and accomplished president than Speaker Peel. In presenting his portrait, I have selected the pose and expression he generally assumed when he called to order some peccant Member; to the discharge of which unwelcome duty I have too often had the opportunity of seeing him compelled to rise.

It is a very curious fact that Members, who are so sensitive about the etiquette of the House, should waste so much time in ignoring it. I recall one evening when an honourable Member ran back to inform the House that a Member so complaining had himself neglected to return the salute of the ever-attentive door-keeper. The one thing that has struck me as peculiar in these remarks in the House is that no Member (so far as I have seen) has gone further than the case of the door-keeper to point to forgetfulness among Members in the House itself. Lookers-on see most of the fight,

THE QUESTION OF THE MOMENT.

'ALL MY OWN WORK.'

Sir Frank Lockwood, Caricaturist Generally, riding his favourite hobby, makes a House.

and, as I was but a looker-on, it was only natural I should notice details that others engaged in the business of the House might miss, and I must say I have frequently been struck with—well, I should not dream of calling it disrespect, but better say forgetfulness, on the part of some Members in saluting the Chair when they leave or enter the House. Certain Members are most careful in making the obeisance. Sir Richard Temple, for instance, must have taken lessons from a professor to perfect himself ; and, although Sir Robert Fowler had more of the brusqueness of the City in his style, he never failed in courtesy to the Chair, in contrast to a few honourable gentlemen seated below the gangway on the other side.

The style of bowing to the Chair is in some cases rather funny. When leaving the benches, Sir Richard Temple, for instance, always stood in front of the gangway, drew both feet together, and bowed low and slowly from the knee. Mr. John Morley does not lose time in this way, but gives a low sweeping step, as if he were about to skate, this step varying a trifle from his usual step in the bow. Others give a sort of friendly nod, while some ignore the salutation altogether. To carry the contrast further, it would be amusing for some Military Member of Parliament to ask whether it is in accordance with the

'SIR RICHARD ADONIS.'

THE PASSING OF PEEL.

etiquette of the House for honourable Members to appear in grey suits (an unheard-of garb in the House ten or twelve years ago). Surely no officer would dare appear on parade in his mess jacket. Nor would an officer dare appear at an inspection wearing a forage cap. Yet, nowadays, Members not only wear grey tweeds (a custom, by the way, Mr. Gladstone was one of the first to adopt), but some honourable Members ignore the orthodox head-gear for a billycock hat, and some are audacious enough to wear the wideawake. But, after all, dress is not so much the question as address, and, in that respect, the military may smile at the civilian Member.

As a specimen of the want of respect for the Chair, I may mention a little incident that happened in connection with Sir Donald Macfarlane. It is difficult to classify Sir Donald. He does not altogether come under the category of bores. He is not quite an eccentric, nor merely a character; he is rather to be placed with members of the don't-care-a-blow-for-anybody type. In fact, he prefers that everyone should have a blow upon his hospitable yacht; but the House is not a private vessel, nor is the Skipper or the Captain to be dictated to. This Sir Donald discovered to his cost, as the accompanying sketch illustrating a little scene with the Speaker, Thursday, February 21, 1895, shows.

THE SPEAKER: In my opinion the ruling to which the hon. Member (Sir D. Macfarlane) refers is entirely inapplicable to the present motion. As I understand, this is an alleged grievance requiring instant remedy.

SIR D. MACFARLANE: Oh! (Cries of 'Order.')

CAUSE AND EFFECT IN THE COMMONS.

The Speaker has modified the unwritten rule concerning the retention of seats by Members. Owing to the prevalence of Influenza, so easily caught by the bare-headed, he suggests that in future, instead of hats, cards may be used to keep places. The cause (the hats) and the effect (the empty House at prayers) are here Kodak'd by our artist.

DIGNITY AND IMPUDENCE.

THE SPEAKER : Order, order! The hon. Member has asked for my opinion, and I hope he will listen to me with courtesy.

At the time the present Speaker was appointed, there was a great deal of excitement about who should fill the chair. Sir William Harcourt was said to envy the post, but, for obvious reasons, he was not the man ; then Campbell-Bannerman was strongly favoured, and it was said that Sir William was the chief cause that he did not get the coveted position. Sir Frank Lockwood was also supposed to be in the running, but the Speaker of the House making caricatures of the Members was too much for some of the Members to contemplate, so Sir Frank had to stand down. I cannot see myself why my own creation of a lady Speakership should not be adopted. Although I introduced Miss Parliamentina merely as a relief in Parliamentary design, there is no reason why a lady in the chair should not become an actuality and a relief to serious work. There are such a lot of old women on the benches of the House, that, for the life of me, I cannot see why a young one should not preside to keep them in order.

But seriously speaking, the Speaker of the House has to work much harder than is generally imagined by those outside, to say nothing of taking part in the various little excursions to the Upper House,

SIR FRANK LOCKWOOD.

where he has to stand at the bar, like a prisoner in the dock.   This interruption of
the business in the House of Commons by the arrival of Black Rod to summon
the Members of the Lower House to the Upper House, to hear the Royal assent given
to certain Bills, will surely soon be altered.   And I trust that my suggestion of the Lord
Chancellor's crier arriving at the door of the House of Commons and calling out 'O
yes, O yes, O yes!   Take notice : the following Bills have received the Royal assent ;'
reading them and retiring, is well worthy of adoption.

A SUGGESTION.

THE SPEAKER IN THE HOUSE OF LORDS.

THE G.O.M.'S LAST SESSION.

GLADSTONE'S last struggle with the Home Rule Bill will ever be remembered as having reduced the House of Commons to something little better than a bear pit. Indeed, the less recorded about the men and matters of Parliament during the Session beginning January 31, 1893, the better.

Neither the men nor the manners of Parliament have improved since April 1886, when Mr. Gladstone first introduced Home Rule. The opening scene on that memorable day was worthy of the occasion, whilst that of the same measure seven years afterwards was unworthy of a drunken brawl at the bar of a pot-house. A free fight took place between the Irish Nationalist Members and Colonel Saunderson and other Tories in the rush for seats. Mr. Gladstone's speech, as was expected, fell far below his great effort in 1886. His voice had gone, and much he said was hardly audible to those even next the table. He was evidently not the man to fight such a battle over again, and to keep in check his Irish allies, who were at fever heat, knowing this effort was to be the last. Indeed, casting aside their small arms, and finding their powder was giving out, the Irish members seized the muzzle ends of their rifles and charged, bludgeoning everyone right and left.

The first attack was upon Lord Salisbury's son-in-law, Lord Wolmer (now Lord Selborne), and the 'Times.' Surely high game! It appears Lord Wolmer had called the Irish Members 'forty paid mercenaries,' and that the 'Times' comments thereon had roused the anger of the mighty Thomas Sexton, and led him to drag these trifles before the House. It was, he said, 'a gross and scandalous breach of the privileges of the House.' Any man of the world would say so too, but then, there are certain Members unfortunately not men of the world.

To make matters worse, the new Government elected a new Chairman of Committees, a worthy gentleman, but, as it soon turned out, a nervous chairman. Poor Mr. Mellor meant well, but a stronger man was wanted in such a stormy session. Other pens than mine have recorded in detail the account of this exciting session. I shall, therefore, merely extract from my Parliamentary Diary the following notes during that time, in the diary form in which I wrote them.

A FEW LEAVES FROM MY DIARY, 1893

March 25.—Mr. Gladstone received quite an ovation on his return to the House last Friday. The Parliamentary performance at Westminster this session is essentially, in theatrical phraseology, a one-part play, and it must have occurred to many to use the hackneyed illustration that 'Hamlet has been acted with the Dane left out.' In consequence of this, all the week, both players and public have shown little interest in the proceedings. To many, the present Parliament is Mr. Gladstone or nothing, and therefore his absence has been more felt than ever before, and his return was a welcome relief. It was remarked that Mr. Gladstone never looked brighter or showed such vivacity as during his brief visit to the House on Friday. But last Monday night, although he had just returned from 'The Durdans,' Lord Rosebery's seat at Epsom, he seemed tired and worn, and his voice was particularly husky. By way of a change, I sat in the Strangers' Gallery, and could hardly hear a word he said. Perhaps he had been discussing the Uganda question *ad nauseam* with the

LORD RANDOLPH CHURCHILL'S LAST SPEECH.

Minister for Foreign Affairs, whose attitude on this important subject gave Mr. Balfour and his followers a rare opportunity for twitting the Premier. Mr. Gladstone shows a partiality for a white flower in his button-hole, an emblem of peace and purity. Green was the prevailing hue in his floral adornment when he introduced the Home Rule Bill, but for the Uganda debate he sported an ominous red flower, presumably to typify the martial attitude he is bound to assume; and, although his voice was not clear, his sarcastic references to Mr. Labouchere's 'generalisation' were sparkling crystals of oratory. Mr. Chamberlain, who wound up the debate, also enjoyed paying Mr. Labouchere back in his own sarcastic coin with compound interest, when he said that

'The Member for Northampton's speech was a very amusing one on a very serious subject, but I do not think a question of international policy ought to be determined by buffoonery.'

April 1.—Last week the most important political episode—outside Parliament—took place when Mr. Gladstone met his supporters at the Foreign Office. It is only a short while ago that the Conservatives met at the Carlton. If this sort of thing goes on, it would be better to give up historical Westminster Hall to these outside conferences. Let it become the playground of the House, but take care not to turn the boys on both sides loose in it at once. Mr. Gladstone's wonderful art was never more apparent than on Monday last. In addition to the impression he made upon his party, whom he raised to a high pitch of enthusiasm, he made a temporary captive at the War Office in the person of Mr. Labouchere, who, when he got up to speak, was beckoned by the Premier to the latter's side in a most fascinating manner ; and in the House itself he was seen at his best when, accepting a glass of water from Mr. Jackson, the perfect light comedy with which he performed this action causing considerable merriment. Whatever one's political opinions may be, it must be admitted by all that by no one can the light touch of Mr. Gladstone be excelled, when it pleases him to play on the softer chords. Lord Randolph Churchill could not find words wherein to express his admiration for the Premier's 'impressive and entrancing' speech ; and this debate, which began as a vote of censure, finished up with a volley of compliments.

April 8.—The Whips of both parties had the greatest difficulty in keeping sufficient Members at St. Stephen's the few days before Good Friday. The weather was aggravatingly fine, and Old Sol did his very best to lure the politicians to fresh woods and pastures new. The fighting men, however, remained, and there was a sharp skirmish on the eve of the holiday. Lord Randolph Churchill rose to the occasion, as his great ancestor would have risen in real battle, and fought in his old dashing style ; and, although dressed in black, he wore brown boots just to show that he was ready for his holiday. It is evident that he 'marks' Sir

THE PREMIER AT BRIGHTON.

MR. GLADSTONE WAITING TO SPRING.

William Harcourt; and, indeed, a little list might be compiled of Members who thus individually 'antagonise' each other. It would run as follows :—

Mr. Gladstone	Mr. Balfour.
Mr. Morley	
Sir William Harcourt	Lord Randolph Churchill.
Mr. Fowler	Mr. Goschen.
All these and the rest of the Gladstonians	Mr. T. G. Bowles.

But this week certainly Mr. Balfour is the political star.

April 15.—Parliament on Thursday re-assembled after the Members' short holiday. There was a great deal of interest and excitement outside the House, but very little inside. The crowd at the gates surpassed in number any I have seen for some time, and Mr. Gladstone received quite an ovation. Inside the House the scene was rather exceptional. Mr. Gladstone spoke to a practically empty House, and indeed there has been very little interest in the doings of Parliament, and very small attendances at St. Stephen's. Dr. Tanner evidently expected something out of the common, for, early in the day, he put in an appearance at the House, apparently with the stock-in-trade of a cast-off-hat merchant. A short time ago the volatile doctor practically broke into the larder of the House of Commons and brought up to the dining-room joints and any eatables he could get hold of. He had a right to this as a member of the Kitchen Committee. Perhaps also he has the entry to the lumber-room, and this miscellaneous collection of head-coverings consisted of those, members had left in the House from time to time when they vanished with a better one. These hats the doctor distributed along the seats, in compliance with the custom of the House as regards securing sitting room ; but the ingenious move of the Nationalist Whip proved needless, for most of the Members were either fishing or golfing, or otherwise enjoying the holiday that Mr. Gladstone endeavoured to curtail. Mr. Gladstone finds Brighton air agrees with him better than the atmosphere of Birmingham or Belfast just now, and, judging from his marvellous vitality last Thursday, ' London by the Sea ' has a wonderful effect upon him. Although personally conducted by Mr. Armitstead, he is mobbed wherever he goes, and some say that public attention is as life-giving to the Grand Old Man as the ozone he breathes. Certainly no statesman displays himself more prominently before the public (and less to his henchmen, it might be remarked) than Mr. Gladstone.

April 22.—The oratorical success on the Irish benches in the debate on the Home Rule Bill has been Mr. Davitt's address: moderate in tone, carefully considered, and

MR. GLADSTONE ATTACKING THE FRONT BENCH.

modestly delivered, it told better in the House than the Ballyhoolyish harangues we are so accustomed to. Mr. Davitt did not give himself away, and his 'reserved force' —to borrow a hackneyed theatrical expression—gave the dramatic effect to his essay, for it was hardly a speech. Like Mr. Blake, Mr. Davitt does not trust too much to memory. Mr. Chamberlain, clear and incisive as usual, made a capital impression against the Bill, and most of the speeches during the week have been from anti-Home Rulers. Sir Ashmead Bartlett broke a long silence in the House, and Mr. T. W. Russell added one more to his many speeches against the Bill. Mr. Leonard Courtney, ex-Chairman of Committees, irritated the Home Rulers by his drastic utterances, and Mr. Chaplin spoke for the ex-Ministers. The last-named gentleman has been a thorn in Mr. Gladstone's side since, twenty years ago, he attacked the figures of the great Chancellor of the Exchequer. He now assailed his facts, and there is no doubt the first Minister of Agriculture has harrowed the Premier's statements with alarming audacity. Mr. Chaplin is a dashing debater; his mind, unlike that of Mr. Labouchere, does not run on Apollinaris, or toast and water, but he can digest stronger stuff, and, with a breezy indifference that is quite delightful, he attacks the Premier with consummate daring. There is no doubt that Mr. Chaplin became a serious politician when he made such a success as Minister of Agriculture, and his speech last Thursday was far in advance of any the Member for Northampton is likely to make. He is not a bitter partisan, and is quite as popular on one side of the House as on the other.

Mr. Goschen's speech on Monday was an excellent specimen of that Member's oratory. The seriousness of this debate is enlivened every now and then by an unconscious touch of humour. For instance, on Monday evening, a Mr. Young, who is apparently over seventy, wound up his maiden speech in favour of Home Rule by declaring that he hoped to live to see a monument erected over the grave of Mr. Gladstone.

April 29.—The Premier, who seems to seek popular acclamation more and more, and who generally meets with an ovation from an admiring crowd at Westminster, when he drives in his open carriage to the House, was taken aback on the eventful Friday by the crowd's suddenly booing at him and shouting 'Traitor! traitor!' They were the Belfast delegates, who had come over for the Albert Hall demonstration on the Saturday; and the extraordinary scene in the Outer Lobby, when the result of the great division was known, was largely caused by this same contingent. More than four hundred policemen were secreted in the building on Friday night, but they remained in ambush. Inside the House the scene was still more extraordinary. Lord Randolph Churchill, at the Constitutional Club, described it as 'a scene of indecent and

MR. GLADSTONE EXCITED.

unrestrained disorder. There was a howling, yelling, bawling, brawling mob, shouting and cheering, not for some great boon they had conferred upon the Empire as a whole, but merely for the gratification of the personal ambition of one man in this country ;' but I recollect that, when Mr. Gladstone was defeated in 1886, it was Lord Randolph who jumped on to his seat and yelled with exuberant delight. Mr. Gladstone, on great occasions, likes, in theatrical phraseology, to 'take the stage' with the limelight full upon him. After the division, instead of coming in casually with the other Members, he waits till the House is full, and then comes from the principal door and walks down the floor through a passage made by a crowd of his supporters, who jump up and cheer vociferously. This reminds me that, at the Constitutional Club, Lord Randolph described the Premier as 'a very elderly *coryphée*,' a not very polite epithet

that will be remembered. It may be a truism that Mr. Gladstone has never delivered himself of any evergreen epigram or startling sentence that will last through time, but all must admit (even Lord Randolph, when he is serious) that he has never said anything that was not delivered with a style and cadence well worth listening to, and a manner that amply repaid the watching. The

M.P.s AFTER A 'SCENE' IN THE HOUSE.

spectacle of this grand old Parliamentary hand at the age of 83 rising in the midst of a crowded and excited Senate at midnight last Friday was one that will for ever linger in the memory of every one fortunate enough to have been present. As an oratorical display it was simply marvellous—a masterpiece of elocutionary power unequalled in our time. This scene has been described by the press *ad lib.*, but one touch I have not seen recorded—the one touch of nature in the Premier's address—his reference to Mr. Chamberlain's son when he mentioned the youthful Member's maiden speech. The firm, pallid face of the parent was turned upon his old chief, and his glassy stare was intense. There was something defiant in that look ; but, when Mr. Gladstone said, 'I will endeavour to sum up my opinion of it by simply saying that it was a speech which must have been dear and refreshing to a father's heart,' the glass

MR. GLADSTONE INDIGNANT.

fell from the eye of the magnate of the Midlands, and Joseph Chamberlain raised his hand to his face and wept.

May 6.—If Mr. Gladstone had been born in the ranks of the idle, he would have been a professional visitor, for he is always staying with some one or other. Mr. and Mrs. Gladstone went from Saturday to Monday to the country residence of Mr. Stuart Rendel, M.P. As regards his London visits, he has deserted Dollis Hill for Hampstead, to which picturesque locality he escapes, when Parliament is sitting, for a breath of the fresh air on our northern heights. At the former place Lord Aberdeen was his host; but, lately, the Premier's son, Mr. Henry Gladstone, has taken a house in the vicinity of 'Jack Straw's Castle,' Hampstead Heath, down a quiet turning hard by the picturesque old house rented by the leaders of the Primrose League, Sir Algernon and Lady Borthwick, where Mr. Gladstone has at times dropped in to have a cup of tea. No doubt some of the narrow-minded members of the Primrose League would be horrified by this little attention on the part of the prominent and active Tories. Indeed, when it was known that, during Mr. Gladstone's last election campaign, he

THE PREMIER AT HAMPSTEAD.

actually drove through beautiful Invercauld, Braemar, at the invitation of Sir Algernon, now Lord Glenesk (who, by the way, was in London at the time), and refreshed himself with a cup of tea, some of the Primrose dames were so aghast at this desecration of the Conservative castle that they actually resigned! This little retreat, in which Mr. Gladstone visits his son, has a row of silent sentries always stationed on the pathway, old inhabitants of Hampstead—the familiar lime-trees, black, branchless, and grotesque in form. I can almost see in them political portraits; the familiar faces which are wont to be fixed on the Premier in Parliament shadowing him at Hampstead.

May 13.—A year ago I met in Washington a well-known politician, who told me he was coming over to England this year to do what I was doing at the time—study the Parliament of the country; and, when I arrived on Monday evening at the House of Commons, I was tapped on the shoulder at the entrance to the Outer Lobby by this gentleman, who had just sent in his card to one of the Members. 'Strange,' he said, when discussing the merits and demerits of our respective Houses of Legislature, 'you've got gas, I see.' 'Oh yes, but we're more advanced in the Inner Lobby and rest of the

EGG-FLIP.

THE LIGHT THAT FAILED.

House—got the electric light,' said his friend, who had just come out to escort him in. Curious to relate, at that moment, as if by magic, the electric light went out, and we were in total darkness. Confusion prevailed in the Inner Lobby, whither Mr. Chamberlain had rushed after one of his onslaughts upon the Government, and nearly fallen over Sir William Harcourt, while Colonel Saunderson all but embraced Mr. Tim Healy. Home Rule, for a time, was in a fog ; and there were not a few who regarded this sudden darkness during the stormy debate upon the Home Rule question as a significant omen. The policemen in attendance ran in with candles, and the American visitor smiled. It was all right in the Legislative Chamber itself, for there is always plenty of gas in the English House of Commons.

May 20.—The Home Rule Bill is having a bad effect on the manners of Members of Parliament, and, if things go on as they have begun, we shall have a series of scenes in the House worthy of the historic fair of Donnybrook in the 'good old days.' The debate has already resolved itself into a single combat between Mr. Gladstone and Mr. Chamberlain. It was generally understood, and, I think, wisely arranged, that before dinner the aged Premier would come down to the House for a few hours in the afternoon, and perhaps occasionally make a speech, and that Sir William Harcourt and his other lieutenants should fight the Bill through. In place of that, we have Mr. Gladstone, as I say, in single combat with the leader of the Unionists ; and the tragic scenes which have taken place during the last week must have plainly shown every one present that the Premier is running a tremendous physical risk. Last Thursday evening, when he worked himself up into a passion

MR. GLADSTONE ELOQUENT.

after the excited and frequently interrupted speech of Mr. Chamberlain, his listeners, twice during his great effort, were alarmed at his spasmodic gasping, which seemed to be a signal that Mr. Gladstone was over-exerting himself. Mrs. Gladstone's face is always an index to the temperament of her wonderful husband, and, after the latter's tremendous tirade, a friend of mine was going up the stairs of the House when he passed Mrs. Gladstone rushing down with a frightened face. She did not notice him, nor anybody, nor anything—her one object was to get Mr. Gladstone away. This she

MR. CHAMBERLAIN.

did, and next day packed him off to the country; and this is the result of only one clause out of the twenty to be passed through the House: On Monday evening Mr. Gladstone and Mr. Chamberlain fought two rounds. Mr. Chamberlain, adopting Mr. Gladstone's tactics of the previous Friday evening, went in to pulverise his antagonist, and he hit very hard when he assured the House of his admiration for the aged Premier. This was followed by a tremendous display of party feeling and ironical cheers from the Irish benches, when Mr. Chamberlain, whom all must acknowledge to be far and away the best fighter in the present Parliament, pointing to the Nationalist Members, said that 'he yielded to no man in the House in his admiration for the Prime Minister. His admiration for his right honourable friend was much more genuine than the recently bought eulogies of honourable gentlemen opposite. His right honourable friend had not paid him for his praise.' No wonder the Irish Members do not love Mr. Chamberlain! It is curious that just at the time Mr. Gladstone was twitting Mr. Cross for his frivolity (which, by the way, was the cause of Mr. Chamberlain's reply), and severely lecturing this new Member for not treating the House seriously, the majority of the Members had turned their backs on the building, and were hanging over the wall of the Terrace to see a pantomime on the river. Captain Paul Boyton was giving a free show to advertise his Water Carnival about to open at Earl's Court, the arena of which, where Buffalo Bill's cowboys mounted and rode their bucking mustangs, and the dusky redskin yelled and flourished his tomahawk, is now a sheet of water. Young ladies and aquatic acrobats were strolling down the Thames in canoe-like water-shoes, and other antics were going on. The band on board the 'Empress Frederick'

A PERORATION.

significantly struck up ' Rule Britannia,' for the special edification of the M.P.s on the Terrace.

June 2.—Parliament resumed on Monday after its brief holiday, and at once plunged into Supply, generally the dullest of all subjects. However, a great many Members turned up, and their attendance was repaid by a lively, if not very edifying, passage of arms—or, perhaps, I should say compliments—between Sir William Harcourt and Sir E. Ashmead-Bartlett. It appears that Sir E. Ashmead-Bartlett has one subject which permeates his whole being, and has for years been smouldering in his breast, even when he was a Junior Lord on the Treasury Bench. This one subject has been weighing heavily upon him—it is the vote for Peterhead Harbour—and now he appealed to the House for some explanation of this all-absorbing topic. This brought up Sir William Harcourt, who scolded Sir Ellis for having dared, as a subordinate Member of the Government, to keep silent instead of coming forward to condemn their conduct, with which he (Sir Ellis) did not agree. He was a bad, wicked boy, and deserved to be severely punished for such hypocrisy. Sir Ellis rose in all the power of his virtuous wrath and indignation, and, pointing to the Chancellor of the Exchequer, exclaimed in a most melodramatic, albeit sarcastic, tone : ' He (the Chancellor of the Exchequer) had no right to rate any one for being inconsistent, considering that he had changed his policy more often than anyone else, and, after swallowing his former opinions, was now revelling in Parnellite juice.' And, in return, he scolded Sir William for his inconsistency during his ' chameleon-like career.' So things are beginning lively, and are likely to continue so.

June 9.—The Home Rule Bill, which is introduced with the object of effecting a union of hearts, promoting of good-fellowship, and generally pouring of oil on the troubled waters, is having the very opposite effect in the House itself. Irritability pervades the whole assembly, and the ' Please, sir, he's calling me names!' ' I didn't say that!' ' You did! you did!' ' I'll tell my big brother!' and all that sort of thing, causes St. Stephen's to resemble a fretful assemblage of school-girls more than ' The best Club in England.' It was therefore unnecessary for the gallant Colonel Brookfield to twit the Members with betting in the House, and just as unnecessary for the accomplished Attorney-General to take the matter up. Things have changed! In ' the good old days ' there was a popular Member of the House known as ' Hippy Damer,' afterwards Lord Portarlington, who, on some important evening, against the wishes of Mr. Gladstone and other Liberals, tried to speak when a big division was coming on. The Government Whip was determined to get him out of the House. There was only one way to do this. The Whip, himself a good sportsman, went behind the Speaker's chair, took out his betting book, and signalled to the irrepressible ' Hippy ' that he

MR. GLADSTONE GAGGED.

wanted to make a bet with him. The massive Member for Portarlington took the bait and went out of the House. I wonder what would be said if that happened now?

On Monday afternoon the House was crammed to hear a question of privilege brought forward by Mr. Chamberlain; it arose, the Member for Birmingham maintained, in connection with two statements in the 'Daily News' of that date; but, with the exception of 'Tay Pay' O'Connor, the whole House agreed that they were intended as a burlesque of the 'News,' and the matter, accordingly, fell through.

June 16.—Is Mr. Gladstone to be gagged? The senior Member for Northampton and the Member for *Bark*shire, better known as Toby, M.P., as well as other Gladstonians, seem to think that the Premier is too voluble. In fact, he is his own obstructionist, and they move the closure upon him. In their opinion, he ought to leave more work to his lieutenants; but, as

I remarked before, the Home Rule Bill is a one-part play, and, when the chief actor leaves the stage, the action ceases, and the piece is in jeopardy. It is a tremendous undertaking for so old a man, and in that fact lies the interest. Take him out of it for a month, and Home Rule is lost for this session. All the committee-rooms would be occupied by the separate parties, holding meetings to consider their differences, with resignations and various squabbles. It is sad to see the Grand Old Man fighting single-handed, but there is no help for it, and gagging him is an impossibility.

The action taken by Mr. Sexton, in throwing up his seat in the House in consequence of a dispute with Mr. Tim Healy over the 'Freeman's Journal,' was received by both sides of the London press with delight. The Gladstonians point to the incident as showing that the Irish party will not be united, but cut up into sections in their Parliament, and that therefore the Ulster men will have equal strength, so that Englishmen ought not to oppose Home Rule any further. At the same time the Unionist press is exultant, pointing to the split as another proof of the absurdity of giving Home Rule to those who cannot agree among themselves. I believe Mr. Sexton was merely bluffing, and that vanity was the sole cause of his attempt at political suicide; just as some strange beings have at one time and another allowed the announcement of their decease to be reported, so as to read the nice obituary notices about themselves. Mr. Sexton, no doubt, is one of the cleverest men in the House. He 'orates,' as Americans say, and deserves his nickname, 'Windbag Sexton.' He is a little man, with a curiously shaped head, small in stature, and wears short trousers. He has a strong belief in Thomas Sexton, and it is no secret that he is anything but popular with his own party.

MR. SEXTON.

June 23.—Who would be a Member of Parliament, with the thermometer 100 deg. in the shade? This has been the most brilliant season since the Jubilee year, and London is surpassing itself in gaiety-garden parties, afternoons, at homes, dinners, balls, receptions, operas, theatrical triumphs, and other attractions too numerous to mention. All can revel in these save one individual—that is the M.P. 'It's downright slavery,' said a Member of the Government to me on Thursday evening (a popular Member whose name has figured in every society function list for years). 'Look here, this is "The Black List" for last week (a list of the attendance of Members of the Govern-

A FULL HOUSE: MR. GLADSTONE UP. *A Sketch from my seat under the Gallery.*

E

ment at division for the week, and for the session, sent to each Member of the Government every Monday), and Mr. Gladstone looked black at me this afternoon, for I am two down. Yes, only missed two divisions, one when I was kept at the office on Government business, and one when some constituents sent into the Outer Lobby for me just before a division. One of them, a stout old dame, fainted in my arms when I told the party there was no chance of getting them in, and before I could shake her off the third bell had gone, and I was just shut out. Dine with you ? Bless me, my dear fellow, I mustn't put my nose outside this House. Look here ! piles of invitations, enough to fill a waste-paper basket daily with them. Ah ! private Members can " pair," but no such luck for the Members of the Government. Slavery is the only word for this state of affairs ; and now Mr. G., as you saw a few evenings ago, acts with his marvellous energy as a " Whip," and watches his party pass the tellers with the eye of a lynx. There can be no exception as long as Home Rule is to the fore. How different it was in previous Governments ! Then there was some *kudos* and some pleasure to be extracted from being a Member of the Government. Now a convict's life is a relief compared to ours ! '

June 30.—It is agreed by all observers of Parliament and its doings that the Tories can cheer better than any other body of men. The Irish Party may, perhaps, be somewhat more demonstrative, but theirs is a yelping, snarling sound. The Gladstonians, again, do not join harmoniously together in one voice ; some in particular are most persistent in giving oral evidence of their feelings. Dr. Farquharson, legs tucked up under his chin, and feet in the back of the bench in front of him, emits a ' Year ! Year ! ' with a cough sandwiched between, that sounds more like a bark than anything else ; and others give vent to their approbation or dissent in sounds more or less effective ; but for a good, sound, hearty, spontaneous, and unrestrained cheer the Conservative benches annex the first prize.

This session, however, they have had no opportunity of displaying their lung power until late on Friday night, when the Scottish Home Rule Bill was defeated, much to the dismay of Sir George Trevelyan, Dr. Hunter, and others. The result was a surprise, and, after the scene, the jaded and worried M.P.s paired for a week, leaving the Estimates to take care of themselves. Next week will be a dull one, indeed, for few Members will put in an appearance at St. Stephen's until Home Rule comes up again for discussion. It is a peculiar coincidence that the vote for the Navy should come on just when we receive the dreadful news of the loss of the ' Victoria ; ' and the powers that be may be prepared for a good deal of discussion by the naval experts in the House, and Lord Spencer, in his capacity of First Lord of the Admiralty, will, in the House of Lords, have to stand the heckling of past naval commanders.

MR. GLADSTONE'S GANG OF SLAVES.

July 7.—Members of Parliament who had paired for the week were brought back to St. Stephen's by Mr. Gladstone's declaration last Wednesday to rush through the Home Rule Bill, and excitement in Parliament has been at fever heat. Mr. Balfour, who had donned the golfer's suit, had to return rapidly to war-paint; but, perhaps, after Mr. Gladstone himself, who has raised his opponents to a state of fury, and intends to fight them single-handed, Mr. Chamberlain has risen in the eyes of the Unionists even higher than before, by the attack he made upon this movement in his speech on Thursday night. I was, unfortunately, not well enough to be present, but I can well imagine the Member for Birmingham, as he wound up his peroration with his glassy eye fixed upon the Irish benches, and quoted the words: 'The snakes committed suicide to save themselves from slaughter.' Those who agree with the Member for Birmingham must surely admit that his speech all through was one of the bitterest and most telling ever delivered by the acknowledged finest debater in the House of Commons. Mr. Balfour also has improved his position as leader during this crisis. There is no denying the fact that the Opposition were at first a little disappointed with his leadership, but this last week showed him to be the right man in the right place; and a prize more to be valued than the most costly gem, viz., praise from Sir William Harcourt for his opponent's moderation, is gratifying indeed. Since no member of the Government replied to Mr. Chamberlain, he was followed by Sir Edward Clarke, who always receives the best attention of the House, for he is a favourite with both sides.

July 11.—Perhaps the most extraordinary scene of disorder and vulgar abuse in the House of Commons took place on the night of July 11. The debate was, of course, about Ireland. It was on the burning question of the number of Members who ought to represent the country. Up to half-past nine the debate was of a perfunctory character ; in fact, these very words were used by Mr. Brodrick in reply to a short speech by Mr. Morley, the Chief Secretary for Ireland. Mr. Brodrick is one of the young men on the Conservative front Bench, not likely at any time to set the Thames on fire or the House of Commons in a blaze; but he very nearly succeeded in accomplishing the latter feat by the following sentence : ' Were the Irish Members to be in greater numbers in that House than others because they represented an impecunious and garrulous race ? ' This remark was seized upon by Mr. Sexton, who rose immediately afterwards and referred to what he (Mr. Brodrick) had said of the Irish race as ' grossly impertinent language.'

Had there been a strong Chairman present (the House was in Committee), five words and five minutes would have sufficed to settle this interchange of compliments. But poor Mr. Mellor could not protect the Chair, nay, as it proved later, could not even protect the Chief Clerk. For exactly an hour and a half he was dragged into one of the most disgraceful wrangles ever known, ending in a free fight. Mr. Mellor ruled Mr. Sexton out of order, and ordered him to withdraw his words. He could not say that the language of the hon. Member for Guildford was out of order, ' but it was very unfortunate.' This weak ruling was just what Mr. Sexton and his friends wanted : wrangling followed. The Nationalists got stronger ; the Chair, with Mr. Mellor in it, creaked under the fury of the opposing parties ; Mr. Mellor was not, in fact, on the chair at all, he was between two stools, and he must eventually fall. He tried to pacify Messrs. Sexton and company by stating that Mr. Brodrick's ' language ' was very provoking, but it was not unparliamentary. Personally, he thought the language used by Mr. Sexton was language he must regret, ' and I hope he will withdraw it.'

Mr. Sexton ' did not want to be offensive,' but at the same time continued to be so.

Lord Randolph Churchill jumped up to say that he thought the discussion very unedifying.

Mr. Sexton retorted that his friend should first withdraw what he had said.

The Chairman thought Lord Randolph's observation a very proper one, and hoped the incident would terminate.

INSIDE THE HOUSE.

SCENE IN THE LADIES' GALLERY.

OUTSIDE THE HOUSE.

MR. A. J. BALFOUR.

Mr. John Morley did not think so. Mr. Brodrick ought to apologise first. This was followed by howls of ' No ! no ! ' and cries of ' Monstrous ! '

Mr. Balfour agreed that the sooner the scene terminated the better ; but he wished to point out that Mr. Sexton had used words (Irish Nationalist Members : 'What were they ? You were not here '). Mr. Balfour had just come in to enjoy the row. Before he could finish his sentence, Mr. Storey rose and tried to take up the running, but Mr. Balfour would not give way. The House howled, and great was the tumult—Mr. Balfour standing, leaning on a dispatch box, moving his mouth and his forefinger in dumb show ; Mr. Storey, with flowing beard, gesticulating, and no doubt speaking, but inaudibly, in spite of his powerful organ, in such a row. The Chairman in dumb show waved to Mr. Balfour to proceed, but as soon as he tried to, up jumped Mr. Storey again, amid calls of ' Name him ! ' ' Name him ! '

Then Mr. Balfour said something, cheered by the Conservatives ; and Mr. Sexton said something, cheered by the Nationalists. Then Mr. Balfour drew forth ' Loud cheers ' by calling for a withdrawal by Mr. Sexton ; and Mr. Sexton drew forth ' Loud cheers ' by repeating the objectionable words.

Then the Chairman rose for the sixth round, but he was getting weaker visibly.

Mr. Evans sprang up to tell the Chairman that Mr. Balfour had shouted out ' Monstrous !' when he, the Chairman, was speaking.

The Chairman (seventh round) appealed blindly to Mr. Sexton to withdraw his naughty words.

Mr. Sexton, speaking as if he were a sovereign, declared, ' We have been subjected to a wanton offence ; are we to humiliate ourselves ? With all respect for your high office, Sir, I must decline to do it.' (Loud cries of ' Name,' and Nationalist cheers.)

High Chair, he evidently intended, for poor Mr. Mellor in his excitement was nearly sitting on the back of his. He had become dazed.

Sir H. James said everybody must wish to avert the scene that seemed likely to take place. He appealed to the hon. Member for Guildford (shouts of ' No ') that he would put himself doubly in the right if he would take the course he would suggest. Might he ask his hon. friend to say that he did not apply the words to any Member of that House ? (Cheers.)

Mr. Timothy Healy said, as he understood, the offensive term was applied to the Irish race. They were described as impecunious and garrulous. That was an insult to the Irish party (cheers), who stood by their countrymen. (Renewed cheers.)

The Chairman : I quite appreciate the feeling of the Member for North Kerry. I think the language used was of a provocative character. The least the hon. Member for Guildford can do is to explain it. I can only express that hope.

Colonel Saunderson said he sympathised with the word impecunious. As to garrulous, it was only another word for eloquent. (Laughter.)

Mr. Timothy Healy : Why, the Member for Guildford himself derives his income from Ireland ! (Great uproar.)

The Chairman : I have requested the hon. Member for North Kerry to withdraw, and I regret that he has not done so in obedience to my request. I disapprove of the language of the Member for Guildford.

There is ruling for you ! In consequence of this childish wobbling, the House got more and more unruly, and a free fight was imminent, when Mr. Gladstone rose. At last the leader of the House thought it time that he should lead. He, in common with every speaker except the Nationalists, spoke of ' supporting the Chair.' Evidently the Chair was weak, but his little speech was provocative in tone and led to further ructions. Here it is : anything but oil on troubled waters :—

NEARING THE END : A HOME RULE CABINET COUNCIL.

LIKA-JOKO

Mr. Gladstone: I regret this occurrence, as to which I derive my information from the language of the right hon. gentleman, the leader of the Opposition. From him I learn that the Member for Guildford used language which was provocative, but not out of order, and that the Member for North Kerry used language in retaliation which was out of order. (A Voice: 'Provocative.') Well, I suppose when you retaliate you do provoke. (Cheers.) I wish to say that I regard it as a first duty to support the Chair (cheers), but I wish to say also that it is my strong, deliberate opinion that the greatest honour will belong to him who is most prompt in bringing the Committee out of its present dilemma. When a disturbance takes place, we are anxious to know who struck the first blow (Ministerial cheers), and, although the first blow may have been short of the one administered in retaliation, yet we do not on that account acquit the person who struck the first blow. On the other hand, I must repeat my words, that in my opinion the Chair ought to be supported (Opposition cheers), and that the Member who assists the Committee out of its difficulty will do himself most honour. If the hon. Member for Guildford is not worthy to stand in that place of honour, I hope the Member for North Kerry will rise. (Cheers.)

This was followed by Mr. Balfour, who made matters worse by stating: I feel bound to say in answer to that, that, if my hon. friend does not rise it is that he is acting on the advice which I have given him. (Great uproar.) It is on my shoulders the responsibility must rest. ('Oh, oh!') The view I take of the matter is this— no doubt the language was provocative, but we are all used to provocative language. I think it will be considered that to say a remark is 'grossly impertinent' is an infringement of the rules of the House. My hon. friend is a member of the nation to which the words were applied. (Mr. Timothy Healy: A stipendiary member.) That is rather provocative language. (Laughter.) &c., &c.

July 14.—A journalist friend of mine has in his chambers a room which he keeps perfectly empty. This he showed me with pride. 'I keep this room,' said he, 'for times when I am over-wrought. Then I shut myself up in it and *roar*. When by this process I have blown away my mental cobwebs, my brain regains its pristine energy, and I go back to my study calm and collected, having done no one any harm and myself a lot of good.' Now it strikes me that the extraordinary scene in the House of Commons last Tuesday when the closure was put on, and the clauses of the Home Rule Bill were 'taken as read,' and voted upon without discussion, suggests that a room should be provided within the Parliamentary precincts wherein M.P.s could—like my journalistic friend—roar themselves hoarse and then vote calmly and peacefully, instead of turning the House into a bear garden. Several Members were so excited that it was a miracle free fights were not indulged in; indeed, some came very near to personal encounters, and are still at fever-heat. The only method I can see of ensuring the safety of our valuable legislators is their adoption—despite the hot weather—of a padded dress when the next evening comes for the 10 o'clock *mêlée*. The Ministers, at least, must get through the ordeal in safety.

July 21.—The Irish are a superstitious race. I wonder in what light they regard the fact that, when Mr. Gladstone was making the important announcement in the House last Wednesday afternoon of his abandonment of the 'In and Out' scheme, and his determination to retain all the Irish Members in the House of Commons, a violent thunderstorm broke over the House and almost drowned the Premier's voice. It can be read in either way by the superstitious. Mr. Stead will deal with the incident in the second number of his new mystical magazine, which treats solely of 'Subjects which are supposed to be beyond the pale of human knowledge.' In No. 1 he gives a portrait of Mr. Balfour ; in giving Mr. Gladstone in No. 2 he might enlighten his ignorant fellow-men upon this curious political coincidence. The eventful Thursday has come and gone, and, like the storm of the previous day, has done little damage. The closured amend-ment voting was tame compared with that of the Thursday before. There were some decided cat-calls in the House, and a visitor in the Ladies' Gallery had to be severely reprimanded for hissing ! The humours of Parliament are scarce indeed, and, if men were endowed with more humour, they would see the ridiculous side of things, and probably never put up for Parliament.

THE GUILLOTINE.

July 28.—Thursday saw the third application of the 'guillotine' to the clauses of the Home Rule Bill, but the House is now accustomed to the beheading process, and even the Chairman of Committees seems to enjoy pulling the string. One effect the 'guillotine' has upon the House is rather curious. The pedestrian exercise caused by the parades through the Division Lobbies has stimulated the athletic proclivities of Members to such an extent, that we are having a regular series of Saturday contests between them at golf, polo, cricket, and all kinds of competitions, including yacht racing. I think prizes ought to be awarded to those quickest through the lobbies when the 'guillotine' is at work.

READY FOR THE FRAY.

ANOTHER SCENE

HOME RULE DEBATE, AUGUST 5, 1893.

THE Home Rule debate waxed warmer as the autumn set in, and fever heat was registered the last evening of the dog days 1893, when the proceedings culminated in a free fight. To use once more a hackneyed expression, 'Members of Parliament are human—sometimes very human,' and it was only human nature that made Pat in Parliament very like Pat in the pothouse (it seems much the same thing nowadays), and the disgraceful scene in the House of Commons on the particular night in question may be attributed to Pat's love for a bit of a shindy. As the base Saxon, Chamberlain, wouldn't fight the excited gentlemen on the Irish benches, they had to fight among themselves, and, in so doing, hit some of the crowd of spectators, who retaliated; and then followed the *mêlée*. The worst feature of all, I think, was the hissing and hooting and execration from the Strangers' Gallery. Members of Parliament have the right, if they like, to turn their House into a pandemonium, to convert 'the best Club in London' into the lowest pothouse; they may get excited and call out 'Judas!' and even more opprobrious epithets; but strangers should recollect that they are not at a penny gaff or a prize-fight, and should show proper respect for our august assemblage. Nevertheless, those in the gallery were but expressing the feelings of the country at the degradation of Parliament.

This happened in Committee, and the Speaker was called into the House to hear from the Chairman of Committees what had taken place. Neither Mr. Gladstone nor Mr. Balfour could enlighten him very much, there being such confusion at the time. Mr. Balfour said that he did not intend to take part in the division, and was not present when the row took place, and, as he said, he was only a reporter of incidents that had come to him by testimony and not by ocular evidence. The Chairman of Committees, at the suggestion of Mr. Timothy Healy, gave his version of the affair, which was also unsatisfactory. Then the Speaker had to address the House, as a headmaster would address a school when there has been a scene in the room, and the chairs and windows have been smashed, and indeed he adopted much the tone of a master in such circumstances.

Mr. O'Connor humbly apologised for any observation of his that might have been the cause of the unseemly state of affairs; and the Speaker accepted the apology in the interest of debate, and in the higher interests of the character of the House, and he asked the House to allow a regrettable incident to pass into oblivion, and to proceed with the business of the rest of the evening in a manner that would do honour to the traditions of the House, and would give no opportunity for enemies of our institutions to rejoice. This caused laughter in the House.

Colonel Saunderson then rose to give his version as follows :—Mr. Speaker, I regret, Sir, to feel it my duty to call attention to a circumstance which occurred after the event which we have just been considering. A sudden charge was made by a number of hon. Members below the gangway on to the seat on which I was sitting. I rose in my place, not desiring to be run over (laughter) by the charge, and the hon. Member for the Ossory Division, without provocation at all, struck me a violent blow on the side of the head. (Nationalist cries of 'No,' and Opposition cheers.) I feel it my duty to call your attention to that fact. I can only say that, so far as that hon. Member is concerned, I gave him no provocation. I never even saw him, until the blow was struck. When I turned round, he was about to repeat it, and he struck me from behind on the side of the head. (Cheers.)

Then Mr. Harrington jumped up amid loud cries of 'Order,' and, when the Liberal Member assured the House that he heard the Serjeant-at-Arms appealing to hon. Members to leave the House, and that he simply came to the assistance of the Serjeant in his endeavours, there were loud laughter and ironical cheers and cries of 'Order.' 'I think, Sir, notwithstanding the laugh, the Serjeant-at-Arms will bear me out—I distinctly saw the hon. Member who has just now complained, before he was struck, strike several hon. Members.' I pity the poor Serjeant that would have to carry out the massive form of Mr. Harrington!

Other Members tried to speak, but the Speaker would not allow the discussion to go on, for any further inquiry would apparently only have revealed the fact that, in the confused *mêlée*, criminations and recriminations took place between Members.

Then there was more from the Chair about dignity and honour, and the Speaker concluded by saying, ' I do not attach blame to any Member. I only ask the House to let the matter drop in the interests of the dignity of the House.' He then left the chair, and at 11 o'clock the division was taken, the Government having only the small majority of 21. The announcement of the numbers was received with loud and prolonged Opposition cheers, louder than ever, because the Members wished to give vent to the feelings which the Speaker had constrained.

On the Monday following there was a general apology for Thursday's disgraceful free fight. The funniest incident was afforded by Mr. Justin McCarthy, who rose to whitewash the Irish Members, and demand from the House what the ' Times ' called ' a formal certificate of character for himself and his friends from the leaders of the great parties of the House,' and he abused the press for making capital out of the *fracas*, and laying any blame on the shoulders of 'the angels of the House '—the Irish Members forgetting altogether that it was Mr. T. P. O'Connor who had caused the row by raising the cry of ' Judas ! Judas !' when Mr. Chamberlain was speaking, and that, until those words were withdrawn, the Opposition had refused to divide, upon which the fight had occurred. Mr. Justin McCarthy also overlooked the fact that Mr. O'Connor, able journalist that he is, made plenty of copy and party capital out of the scene—a scene, Mr. Balfour reminded the House, that has not had a parallel in Parliamentary history for upwards of two hundred years.

August 25.—Members of Parliament have run back to town this week for the last round of the stand-up fight between the Premier and Mr. Chamberlain, for that is really what the important political crisis has come to. It is not to be a fight 'to a finish ; it is to be closured and renewed when the Bill is brought up another session. But phew !—who wants to dwell on politics in such weather as this ?

MR. KEIR HARDIE.

September 1.—The London season is dead and buried, and Parliament is all that remains to talk or write about. Even that is dull beyond description. The jaded legislators are yearning for fresh air, and even the approaching final division on the Home Rule Bill has failed to arouse more than a languid interest. I felt this depression last Friday evening when I entered the Lobby, its sole occupants being the tired-out door-keepers and the leg-weary policemen. I really believe a swarm of wasps would not have roused them to activity, for I noticed a bluebottle lying undisturbed upon the nose of one of Inspector Horsley's staff. I sought the Terrace, which, by the way, has been rousing the ire of

Mr. Keir Hardie, who has been picturing to his friends in the north the bloated aristocrat here wasting his time with his fair friends in the enjoyment of strawberries and cream, and tea and cake. Perhaps it will interest Mr. Keir Hardie to know that, when I was on the Terrace last Friday afternoon, only one Member was enjoying tea and cake with a lady; and that was one of the working men's representatives in Parliament, who, earlier in the session, brought down three or four lady friends to tea on the Terrace, and, being impatient for the strawberries and cream, those delicacies so iniquitous in the eyes of Mr. Keir Hardie, actually took those from another Member's table, and assisted his friends to finish them off!' This was witnessed by me in the presence of the editor of a London evening Radical paper, who severely commented on the greediness and lack of manners on the part of one of his beloved ones.

END OF HOME RULE BILL

HOUSES OF COMMONS AND LORDS, SEPTEMBER 8, 1893.

AT last the discussion on the Home Rule Bill came to an end, and, when the division was taken, there was a sigh of relief in St. Stephen's to think that we had seen the last of the Home Rule Bill for some time at least. The curtain was a poor one; in fact, the whole of the last act dragged. The facetious Dr. Wallace made a long address, but it fell flat after his splendid effort a few weeks before. Mr. Chamberlain was vigorous and effective, as usual, but neither Mr. Balfour nor Mr. Morley rose to the occasion; Mr. Gladstone, after the division, which proved he had a majority of thirty-five, sat tranquilly enough at the bench writing to Her Majesty to inform her that he had at last forced the House to carry the Bill. The cheers that came from the gentlemen on the Irish benches were, indeed, feeble in the extreme; as I say, it was a mere sigh of relief rather than a tremendous triumph. The humours of Parliament are inexhaustible! To get this Home Rule Bill printed for the Lords, and allow the Peers to return to their partridges, it was necessary to read it the first time immediately it passed the Commons. Only five Peers had sat up to act this little farce, and a dozen words were all that were spoken. The fun would have been complete when Earl Spencer moved that the Bill be read a first time had half a dozen Conservative Peers dropped in casually and demanded a division upon it. The Government would have been defeated, and five minutes would have sufficed to have thrown out Home Rule. What a pity this hadn't been arranged! Meanwhile the Commons escaped from

SCENES IN THE HOUSE OF COMMONS: III. QUESTION TIME. *Sketch from my seat under the Gallery.*

London without delay. The first to go was the Hon. E. Blake, the Nationalist Member for South Longford, who ran off, the moment his vote was recorded, to catch the newspaper train *en route* for Queenstown and Canada. No doubt he was gratuitously supplied with all he required to read. One would like to know what his thoughts were upon the Bill to support which he had given up his splendid career in Canada. If all we hear is true, he was heartily sick of the whole thing. More than one of his colleagues disgusted him ; for he is too experienced and important a politician to throw in his lot with the rough material from Ireland that sits around him.

The Home Rule Bill was killed by ridicule. After its sensational passage through the Commons, it was duly presented in the Lords. Lord Rosebery, indeed, suggested that the poor thing caught cold in the corridor between the Houses, and was dying of the effect of the chill before Earl Spencer apologised for its appearance ; and it was Lord Rosebery who chaffed rather than defended the measure. Still the Opposition were not in the humour to treat the matter as a joke. As a literary and histrionic triumph, the Duke of Argyle's speech ranks with that of Dr. Wallace in the Commons. I regret to say I did not hear it ; but I was in at the death, and I shall never forget the splendid spectacle the House of Lords presented on that memorable evening ; it was the largest and most distinguished House on record, dealing with the largest and most important question brought before the Peers at any time. The scene was worthy of an historic night. The Peers crowded the seats ; the Bishops in their robes on the benches, and the Duchesses in their splendid dresses in the galleries, added a unique effect to a Parliamentary debate. The Commons stood by the throne and were packed under the gallery. Not a seat was vacant. They heard Lord Cranbrook, the dashing debater they knew so well in the Commons as Gathorne Hardy, deliver a speech quite worthy of his fighting days. They heard the Lord Chancellor, in wig and gown, plead with unusual energy for the bantling of the Cabinet ; they heard the thunder of Lord Salisbury, and saw the Chamber lit up with the flashes of the sarcastic lightning ; and they yawned at Lord Kimberley's reply. The House was literally and figuratively at fever heat when, at seven minutes past midnight, the Lord Chancellor put the eventful question, ' That this Bill be now read a second time.' ' Content ! ' was the scarcely audible cry from the Government benches. ' *Not* content ! ' was the roar from the rest of the House. None but a Lord Chancellor could have said what Lord Herschell did at that moment. He actually gave it as his opinion that the ' Contents ' had it—a solemn and formal announcement that was received with laughter from all sides. It took the ' Non-contents ' half an hour to pass out and record their votes, a few minutes sufficed for the supporters of Home Rule to do likewise ; and when the Lord Chancellor announced the numbers—41 for and 419 against—the Peers did not jump up and wave their hats and shout themselves hoarse and cry ' Judas!' or yell at their opponents, or cheer their leaders. Nothing of the sort ; they laughed loud and long. They killed the Home Rule Bill with ridicule.

Did, or did not, a lunatic Lord vote against the Home Rule Bill in the division of the House of Lords ? That was the question which was propounded immediately that the House of Lords threw out the Bill, by that section of the press which panders to the lower strata of society by providing personalities daily, in an all-hot, two-a-penny style. Well, suppose a lunatic did vote ? Surely the opposing papers catering for the same public may fairly ask, ' How many lunatics voted in the House of Commons ?' How many editors assured their readers that Mr. Gladstone was nothing but a lunatic to introduce such an insane Bill as the Home Rule scheme ? And how many informed their subscribers that Lord Salisbury ought to have been locked up in Bedlam, as a dangerous maniac, for having thrown out such a splendid settlement of the Irish difficulty ? During the heated and undignified session the word ' Lunatic!' was frequently heard in the House and read in the political articles; so the noble light-headed Lord may well be left alone. The Lower House, instead of trying to reform the House of Lords, might well have taken a leaf out of the latter's book, as anyone would have admitted who was fortunate enough to be present during the debate on the Home Rule Bill. Both Houses were sick and tired of the whole question, and on the following Thursday, for the space of one minute, Sir William Harcourt was the most popular man in the House of Commons. That was when he stood up to move that, when the House rose on the following day, it should stand adjourned till November 2. The hearty cheering that followed this statement was contributed to by every Member present, and, unlike most ' general cheering,' which is, as a rule, semi-ironical, this was genuine.

The doors of St. Stephen's then closed, and London was quit of the unruly gentlemen who were wont to disport themselves therein.

'LUNATICS.'

WILLY BOY, WILLY BOY.
(THE G.O.M.'s RESIGNATION.)

'*Willy boy, Willy boy, where are you going?*'
'*I am tired, 'tis the end of the day,*
I stayed at St. Stephen's and helped with the sowing,
But now they are all making hay.'

IT cannot be said that Mr. Gladstone leaves any school of politicians behind him. All other leaders have impressed younger statesmen to such an extent that they have either consciously or unconsciously imitated them. Even Lord Iddesleigh had in the House quite a following of junior politicians who imitated his peculiar Parliamentary manner—the reason being, possibly, that Sir Stafford in the House of Commons had the best style of ' House of Commons manner' in our time. Mr. Gladstone, on the other hand, has too strong an individuality for anyone to attempt to imitate. He prided himself on being reticent and keeping his own counsel in his Parliamentary work, and, although he would willingly reply to any correspondent on any subject he might write to

THE GRAND OLD BABY ENJOYING TIM'S ANTICS.

(*According to Mr. Dillon, M.P., the revolt of Mr. Timothy Healy ' would not frighten a baby.'*)

him about, when it came to his tactics in Parliament, he was a sphinx. In fact, on the memorable occasion in 1889, when flung back into Opposition, he rose in the House, and, turning round to the younger Members sitting behind, who had just been returned to support him in opposition, he held up his hand and asked them, as an old Parliamentary hand, to take his advice and follow his example in keeping their own counsel until the occasion when it would be profitable to make public their intentions. It was then the phrase 'an old Parliamentary hand' originated ; and I may be pardoned for repeating here that it was I who, *à propos* of this remark, drew public attention for the first time to the fact that, although Mr. Gladstone used the expression 'an old Parliamentary hand' figuratively, in reality the left hand he held up while he spoke those words, had

THE WELSH ROCKING STONE.

Another hypnotic experiment at Westminster. Professor Merritt Morley puts the Home Rule Bill in a trance for the Session.

but three fingers. I happened that evening to be the guest of a club of journalists, and, speaking of English caricaturists as compared with those of other countries, I said it was to the credit of those in this country that they did not seize upon the deformities of public men for ridicule. For instance, Mr. Gladstone had that after-noon spoken of the old Parliamentary hand. Were I a foreigner, I should at once have utilised that remark by drawing the hand of Mr. Gladstone, showing it as it is, with one finger gone (Mr. Gladstone had for years worn a black patch on the left hand to conceal the loss of the finger), and might have been tempted to show that the finger missing had something to do with Home Rule. Now this comment of mine made public for the first time, as I say, that Mr. Gladstone was deficient of a finger; and yet Members who had sat in the House with him for twenty years had never noticed it! So much for observation. So much for the criticisms of those who, like Mr. Labouchere, fail to see the peculiarities of Members on his side of the House when pointed out by caricaturists unprejudiced by party feeling. After this, of course, every artist all but labelled the black patch on Mr. Gladstone's left hand, just as they honoured me by taking my type of Mr. Gladstone generally, including the collar, and adopted my Harcourt, my Churchill—in fact, my bag of Parliamentary tricks, which I, as the first artist to attend the House regularly, to depict it realistically, got together for my journalistic work. Still, I must admit that these Parliamentary caricaturists have given a much better impression of Mr. Gladstone, and other politicians, than can ever be gathered from the conventional portraits manufactured merely from photographs.

There was a tragic suddenness in Mr. Gladstone's leaving the House. He was far from Parliamentary second childhood, and neither Mr. Timothy Healy nor anyone else could frighten him. He was still the energetic personality, he was still the rocking stone ; with a wag of his head he moved the whole of the Welsh vote, with a wag of the finger he still directed the Nonconformist conscience. He had his humorous eye open also. The story of the Grand Old Man's cheque showed that, and even the Redmond-Parnell Home Rule Quartette sang his praises ; but he vanished, and with him Home Rule.

Mr. Morley, Mr. Gladstone's ardent lieutenant, was obliged to put it to sleep. I wonder now whether the Grand Old Man thinks of these days of obstruction, of slavery to his Irish friends, a yoke he carried to the close of his Parliamentary career. Shall those days ever be forgotten ?

THE IRISH YOKE.

*He's gone, and she knows, like a faithful auld hound,
    Who forgets not the joys or the wars of the past,
In youth or in age, grief or grandeur, he's found
    Still loyally loving, and true to the last!*

BEFORE THE BALL.

LORD ROSEBERY, M.C., *loq.*—'*Here's a pretty state of things: all these ladies to be looked after, and I've got two lovely black eyes and a broken nose!*'

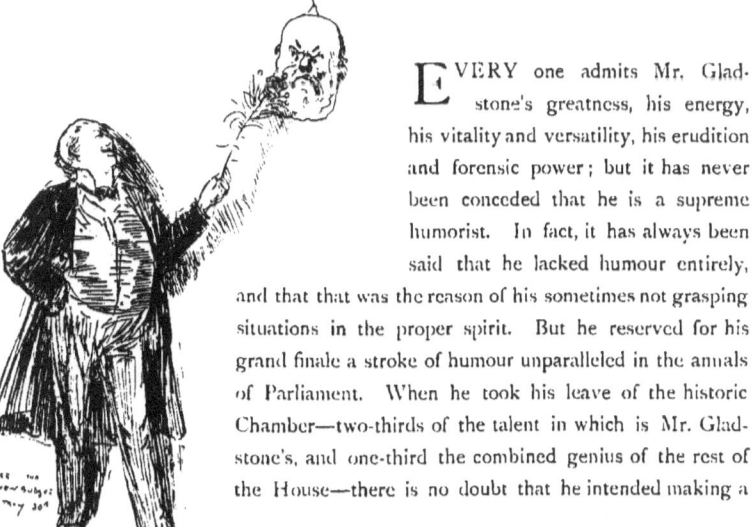

SEE THE NEW BUDGET MAY 30th

EVERY one admits Mr. Gladstone's greatness, his energy, his vitality and versatility, his erudition and forensic power; but it has never been conceded that he is a supreme humorist. In fact, it has always been said that he lacked humour entirely, and that that was the reason of his sometimes not grasping situations in the proper spirit. But he reserved for his grand finale a stroke of humour unparalleled in the annals of Parliament. When he took his leave of the historic Chamber—two-thirds of the talent in which is Mr. Gladstone's, and one-third the combined genius of the rest of the House—there is no doubt that he intended making a grand *coup* in his resignation of the Premiership. The leaking out of the piece of news, which was snapped up and made public by the new journalism, prevented this. But the House was crowded to hear what was felt to be his farewell speech; a speech that would doubtless touch upon many questions, and probably avoid that upon which it was felt that Mr. Gladstone was not in accord with some of the members of his party—namely, the attack upon the House of Lords. Yet, to the surprise of all, this last speech was a violent onslaught upon that body. Now comes the humour of it. Mr. Gladstone nominated for the Premiership a Member of the House of Lords, Lord Rosebery, who has never sat in the Commons! Lord Rosebery, in the circumstances, could not refuse the Premiership, although it is well known to his friends that he was a Home Ruler not by conviction, but by accident. When that important question was first made the question of the hour by Mr. Gladstone, Lord Rosebery, like Mr. Fowler and others, sat on the fence, and was undecided upon which side to jump, until someone made a remark to him privately that piqued him; then he lent his name to Home Rule. Had that friend not chaffed him, he would have sat probably with the Duke of Devonshire. One reason that made Lord Rosebery a fitting successor to Mr. Gladstone was, that we did not lose the Premier's collars; for, though Mr. Gladstone's collars flaunted wildly in the breeze, the grand young man affects collars quite as large in dimensions as those of his equally grand, but more ancient chief. Instead of possessing wings, however, Lord Rosebery's collars are upright; but both Parliamentarians, to use a yachting technicality, 'carry the same amount of canvas.'

Lord Rosebery is in appearance particularly youthful, with his full round face, well-cut mouth, and light eyes. He has a clear, easy delivery, and a great command of epigram and diction, in strong contrast to Lord Kimberley, whose place Lord Rosebery took as Leader of the House of Lords, to which position Lord Kimberley has lately returned. There is nothing prosaic about Lord Rosebery. Like the great chief he succeeded, he is full of surprises; and the greatest of all was his casual remark about Home Rule, to the effect that he agreed with Lord Salisbury, that, until there was a majority in England in favour of the measure, it would not, in his opinion, be justifiable.

If the matter in the new Premier's first speech was attractive, so likewise was his manner. He began well and made a most favourable impression on all sides. His preliminary canter at the Foreign Office, before the House met, on the day on which he first appeared as Premier in the House, showed that he was well trained for the political race, for which he had been made so strong a favourite. Indeed, he made all the running in the debate which followed in the House of Lords.

All have heard of the youthful bet of the ex-Premier, in which he declared to

THE EIGHTH LORD ROSEBERY: AS THE G.O.M.

A poor performance, though! And mark that where
The master would himself himself forswear,

The pupil uses puppets to unsay:
He pulls the strings, and they explain away.

[BEFORE HE WENT TO SHEFFIELD.

marry the heiress of her season, become Prime Minister of England, and own the winner of the Derby. These feats he accomplished, and there seems every likelihood of his repeating the same feat. It is not known, however, that he made another bet of a triple character. One item was, that he would pacify the Irish party without giving them Home Rule ; another, that he would bring back the Unionists to the Liberal fold ; and the third, that our hereditary legislators would have to evacuate the Upper House, and give up the historic Chamber to the meetings of the London County Council.

THE ROSEBERY PARLIAMENT.

LORD ROSEBERY is a veritable Crichton. A statesman, an orator, a historian, a wit, a society *raconteur*, a sportsman, an organiser, a thousand and one things. It is not to be wondered at, therefore, that he gives many a chance a less versatile man could not to the captious critics and the caricaturist, and in the latter capacity I subscribe the following sketches, which perhaps sum up the growth of his genius, and which, I am sure he will be satisfied, were never designed, nor are they here reproduced, as anything but the fairest criticisms by one who is, apart from his Parliamentary position at the time, one of Lord Rosebery's greatest admirers.

Perhaps the only series in this collection that I might be expected to refer to, after the few remarks I have made in the preface, is that relating to Lord Rosebery's Premiership. I have had the honour of Lord Rosebery's acquaintance for some time, and, like all who come in contact with him, however slightly, have found him a most delightful and accomplished man.

It is simply a fact that these drawings and cartoons, which I here reproduce, were honest criticisms of Lord Rosebery's public position at the time—a position which events have shown he did not relish ; and were I now to publish cartoons dealing with him, I would show him to be what no doubt he is, the man of the future of the Liberal Party. I had to deal with his political past, a past that he will, I am sure, be glad to forget ; and, if he has ever seen my caricatures, he will let the impression they made— if they did make any—vanish with the mass of criticism published at the time, from mutual friends wielding a pen far stronger than I do a pencil.

TEN LITTLE ROSEBERYS.

ONE little Rosebery doffing Eton blue,
Went up to Oxford, then there were two.

Two little Roseberys didn't take degree,
Sent down for racing, then there were three.

Three little Roseberys on their native shore,
Guiding of the G.O.M., then there were four.

Four little Roseberys in a hornet's hive,
Took the chair at L.C.C., then there were five.

Five little Roseberys, tired of Vestry tricks,
Wrote a life of Mr. Pitt, then there were six.

Six little Roseberys heralded as heaven—
Born to Foreign Office stool, then there were seven.

Seven little Roseberys very up-to-date,
Arbitrated coal strike, then there were eight.

Eight little Roseberys very large and fine,
Winning of the Derby, then there were nine.

Nine little Roseberys, merry little men,
Making funny speeches, then there were ten.

Ten little Roseberys, trying on their fun,
With the Constitution, then there were—None.

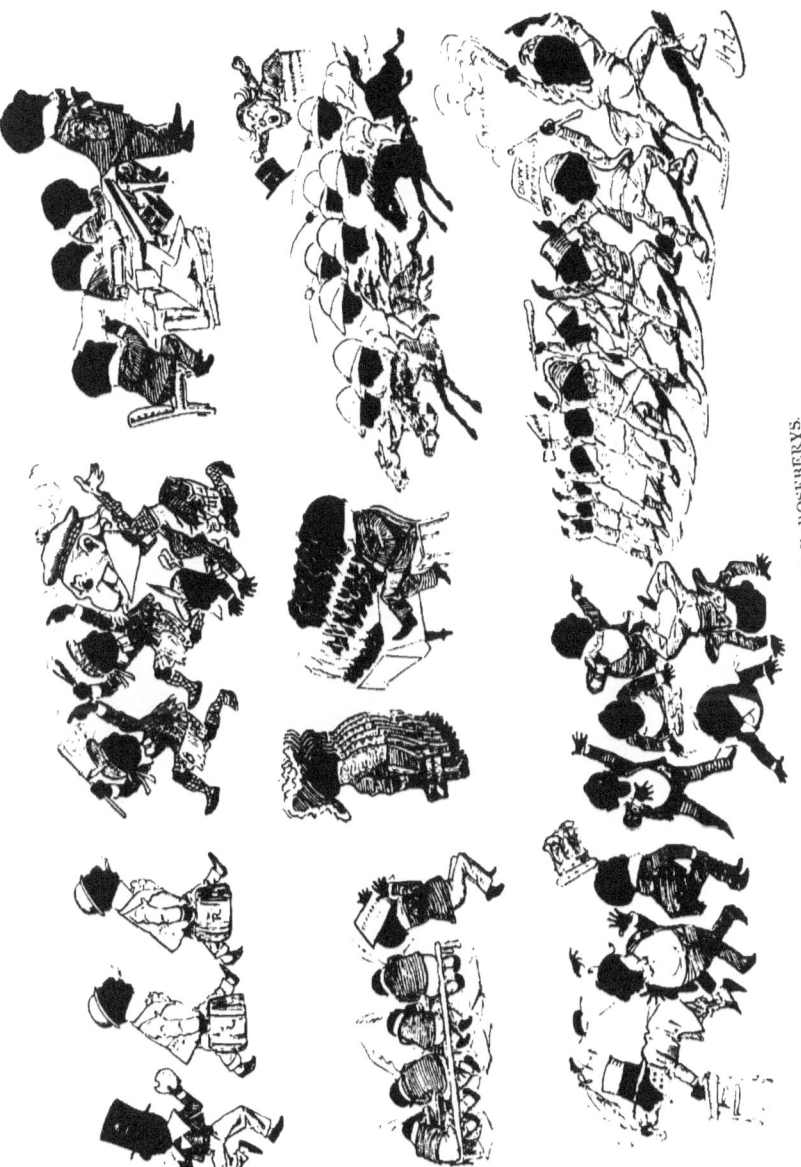

TEN LITTLE ROSEBERYS.

THE AWAKENING OF ROSEBERY.

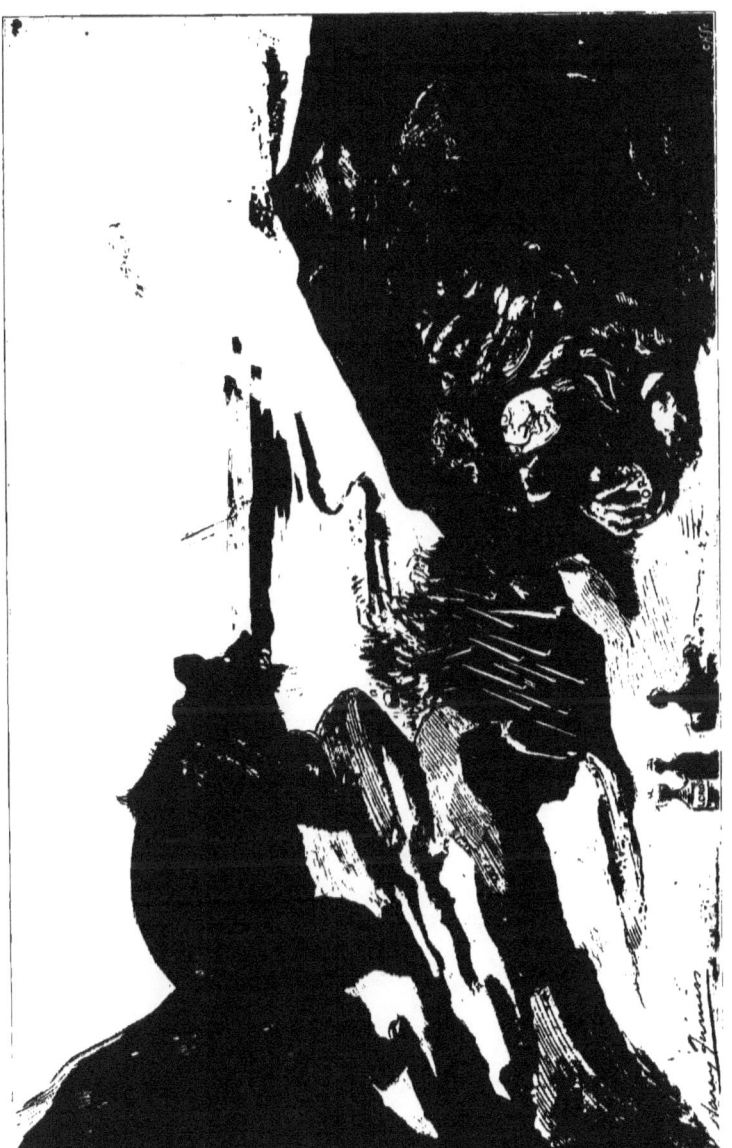

NOVEMBER, 1894

THEIR LAST BOAT.

HARCOURT (*First Mate*): '*Keep 'em back, there.' keep 'em back.' If we take any more they'll sink us.*'

'PLOUGHING THE SANDS.'

JOHN BULL: 'Here, I say, what are you doing there?' "Ploughing the sands?" Come, come, quit this tomfoolery and do some work that is likely to lead to crops.'

THE GOVERNMENT PLATFORM.

RETIRED—HURT!

MISS PARLIAMENTA has no greater favourite than Sir William Harcourt. He is always excellent company and most entertaining, and, shall I say, amusing when in his most serious mood?

Sir William has been in a bad temper for a period extending over the last two sessions, and there is no doubt whatever that he has every reason to be in a bad temper, and the sympathy of the House is with him, for Sir William has been the most unfortunate of men. Probably no

H

REDUCING THE MAJORITY BY ONE.
The Exit of Dr. Macgregor.

politician has worked harder and gained less, and that has doubtless made him in a bad temper.

Angry as Sir William was in the House, he was childlike and bland temper compared with Sir William on the stump. The Veto

'FOAMING POWDER' AFTER THE DECLARATION OF THE POLL.

Bill lost him his seat—of that there is no doubt. It was evident that capital would be made out of the fact of Lord Rosebery's winning his two Derbys and losing two seats at Derby, and I

SHAKING THE SAWDUST OUT OF
SIR DONALD MACFARLANE.
See page 102.

had made a sketch of Lord Rosebery's nightmare when I took up the 'Globe' the same evening and found the following lines in 'By the Way':—

> ''Twixt ups and downs and outs and ins,
>   Life has its little crosses :
> The man who scored two Derby wins,
>   Must bear two Derby losses.'

Nothing daunted, Sir William sent the following memorable telegram : 'I shall per-

*'I shall persevere as long as I am able in the Liberal cause and the maintenance of
the principles to which I am attached.'*

SIR VETO: THE DERBY LOSER.

PUNCTUATING THE BUDGET.

The Crown Derby Chin-a
'Historicus' Mug, slightly
damaged, and imperfectly
cemented.

severe as long as I am able in the Liberal cause and the
maintenance of the principles to which I am attached,' and
struck an attitude which I have endeavoured to portray on
the preceding page.

On another page I refer to a 'scene' between the
Speaker and Sir Donald Macfarlane, who was called to
order. Two months afterwards the effect of this quiet
reprimand from the Captain wore off; he then went for
the Skipper Harcourt. Sir William was in command, riding
out a stormy session, when the Scotch Members became
uneasy about their little Bills, and brought all the pressure
they could to bear upon the leader to give more attention
and time to them. Shouting at Skipper Harcourt, Sir

A BACK VIEW—THE CHANCELLOR OF THE EXCHEQUER.

Donald asked in tones that could be heard above the storm and tumult, 'Is not the right hon. gentleman aware that if any further delay occurs, the Scotch Members will have to reconsider their action in support of the Government?'

There was a startling bluntness in thus so coarsely defying the Government, that any one else would have shrunk from. It would have been easy to imply as much in another way, and probably the effect would have been better. As it turned out, Sir

William 'went for' Sir Donald as a dog would go for a doll, and shook the sawdust out of him. The leader was furious, and, if not in words, certainly by withering contempt, told Sir Donald he did not care a great big D about him or his friends or their support.

It was soon after this that that eccentric Member, Dr. McGregor, the *farceur* of the Scotch contingent, was so much in evidence. It is hardly necessary to recall the tit-bits of this peculiar senator's sayings. He was always interrupting the business of the House at the most inopportune moments, but let it be recorded that it was on Monday, May 18, 1895, when the Rosebery government was tottering in its decline, that the mighty McGregor arose and assured Her Majesty's Ministers, sitting upon the Bench in the House of Commons, that, if they did not at once acknowledge the McGregor as their Dictator, he would withdraw his support and the Government would collapse, and he gave the Government until the following Tuesday to decide upon their fate. The question was put to the Leader of the House, who gave an evasive reply. 'That isn't good enough for me,' roared the McGregor, and, throwing a withering glance at Sir William Harcourt, he strode out of the House. In due course the Government vanished, and the country, remembering this incident, decided that that Government should not return for many years to come. *The McGregor was avenged.*

Sir William at one time imagined himself becoming Lord Chancellor, but that post was already filled, and when it seemed that the time at last had come for his many many years of hard work in the Commons to be rewarded by the Premiership, Lord Rosebery stood in the way; and most Members on both sides of the House considered that Sir William was hardly fairly treated. Lord Rosebery was Mr. Gladstone's pet. Can there be anything in the retort that the Grand Old Man looked upon Sir William as his Pecksniff? Could he have, in his library, come across the following passage in 'Martin Chuzzlewit'?—

'Time and tide will wait for no man,' saith the adage. But all men have to wait for time and tide. Mr. Pecksniff had in this respect endured the common lot of men. 'An uncommon lot of that common lot,' Mr. Pecksniff opined.

That tide, however, which taken at the flood would lead Mr. Pecksniff on to fortune, was (of course) marked down in the table, and seemed about to flow. No idle Pecksniff lingered far inland, unmindful of the changes of the stream; but there, upon the water's edge, over his shoes already, stood the worthy creature, prepared to fling himself full length upon the flood so soon as it should slide towards the quarter of his long deferred hopes.

'And who shall blame him?'

The likenesses sent him of his two fair daughters (Torry and Whiggy, as they were affectionately nicknamed) were comically touching indeed. They had a virginal resemblance to show their parent's manly physiognomy, combined with separate and individual differences of expression, manner, and bearing, which, on a typical illustration of identity underlying diversity, must have been of peculiar interest to a modern Darwinian anthropologist. Heredity in all its phases *is* so interesting.

They had that firm reliance in their parent's nature—a parent who seemed almost more like a genial brother or sympathetic cousin, than the typical austere and pompous paterfamilias—which taught them to feel certain that in all he did, he had his purpose straight and full before him. And that its noble end and object was himself, which, of necessity, included *them*, they knew. The devotion of these maids was perfect.

One morning, Mr. Pecksniff appeared with a breathless rapidity, strange to observe in him, at other times so calm ; and, seeking immediate speech with his daughters, shut himself up with them in private conference for two whole hours. Of all that passed in this period, only the following of Mr. Pecksniff's utterances is known :—

'HISTORICUS' WEEPS.

'How he has come to change so much and so quickly (as he says he has) we needn't stop to inquire. My dears, I have my thoughts upon the subject, but I will not impart them. If he wants our friendship he shall have it. We know our duty, I hope.'

That same day an Old Gentleman sought an interview with Mr. Pecksniff.

Though the face and form and gait of this Old Man, and even his grip of the stout, if somewhat worn, umbrella he carried, and on which he leaned, were all expressive of a resolution not easily shaken, and a purpose (it matters little whether right or wrong just now) such as in other days might have survived the rack, and

had its strongest life in weakest death, still there was now, as it were, a certain air of martyrdom in his demeanour.

. . . .

'Your daughters are well?' said the Old Man, laying down his hat and umbrella.

Mr. Pecksniff endeavoured to conceal his agitation as a father, when he answered, 'Yes, they were.' They were good girls, he said, very good. And generally considered remarkably to 'favour' their sire. He remarked that there was an easy chair in the room, and that the door was far from being air-tight. The latter imperfection, he might perhaps venture to add, and *others*, were not uncommonly to be met with in old houses.

The Old Man sat down in the easy chair, and, after a few minutes' silence, said :—

' It is not my habit to put my—well, my friends to so much sudden trouble to gratify my—well, say caprices !'

' *Caprices*, my good sir !' cried Mr. Pecksniff deprecatingly.

' That is scarcely the proper word either, in this instance,' said the Old Man. ' No, you are right. It is not a caprice. It is built up on reason, proof, and cool comparison. Caprices never are. Moreover, I am not a capricious man, I never was.'

' Most assuredly not,' said Mr. Pecksniff.

' The intentions I bear towards you now ' (pursued the Old Man) ' are—well, perhaps such as you may divine.'

Mr. Pecksniff moved his hands deprecatingly. ' Deserted by many whom I most trusted ' (continued the Old Man), ' flouted and beset by many who should help and sustain me, I fly to you for refuge. I confide in you to be my ally ; to attach yourself to me by ties of Interest and Expectation '—he laid great stress upon these words, though Mr. Pecksniff particularly begged him not to mention it—' and to help me to visit the consequences of the very worst species of meanness, jealousy, dissimulation, and vindictiveness on the right heads.'

' My noble sir !' cried Mr. Pecksniff, catching at his outstretched hand. He looked up to the ceiling, and clasped that hand in rapture.

.   .   .   .

' Your daughters,' said the Old Man, after a short silence. ' Are they like you ? '

' In the nose of my elder, and the chin—some rudely say *chins*—of my younger,' began the widower, ' some say their parent lives again.'

' I don't mean in person,' interrupted the Old Man. ' Morally—morally.'

''Tis not for me to say,' retorted Mr. Pecksniff, with a gentle smile. ' I have done my best, sir, to ensure a—so to say—*a moral continuity and spiritual consistency* in—in—the inevitable mutabilities of time and chance and natural development.'

' I could wish to see them,' said the Old Man. ' Are they near at hand ? '

They—the daughters—grouped themselves about the Old Man's chair, and hung over him.

The Old Man looked attentively from one to the other, and then at Mr. Pecksniff several times.

They *were* singularly like each other and their sire. Yet with marked and significant divergences nevertheless. The elder showed a *soupçon* of aristocratic—not to say Tory—*hauteur*, the younger a trivial touch of chilly—not to say Whiggish—reserve, both which characteristics were at the present moment markedly absent in their roseate and rotund, not to say Radically, robustical parent.

'Tory and Whiggy, eh?' murmured the Old Man, repeating them after Mr. Pecksniff. 'Terms of familiar family endearment, doubtless. I shall not easily forget them.

.   .   .   .   .   .

'Do you never sit down, Mr. Pecksniff?' asked the Old Man suddenly.

'Why, yes, occasionally sir,' replied Mr. Pecksniff, who had been standing all this time.

'Will you do so now?'

'Can you ask me,' returned Mr. Pecksniff, slipping into a chair immediately, 'whether I will do *anything* that you desire?'

'You talk confidently,' said the Old Man, 'but I fear you hardly know what an old man's humours are. You don't know what it is to be required to count his likings and dislikings; to adapt yourself to his policies and prejudices, to do his bidding, be it what it may; and always still be zealous in his service.'

'We always said—my girls and I—' cried Mr. Pecksniff with increasing obsequiousness, 'that, while we mourned the heaviness of our misfortune in being confounded with the time-serving and unnecessary, still we could not wonder at it. My dears, you remember?'

'Oh, vividly! A thousand times!'

'We uttered no complaint,' said Mr. Pecksniff. 'Occasionally we had the presumption to console ourselves with the remark that Truth would in the end prevail, and Virtue be triumphant, but not often. My love you recollect?'

'Recollect? Could he doubt it? Dearest pa, what strange, unnecessary questions!'

'Ah!' pursued the Old Man, 'you have also said much more, which, added to other circumstances that have come to my knowledge, opened my eyes. You spoke to me, disinterestedly, on behalf of ——. I needn't name him. You know whom I mean.'

Trouble was expressed in Mr. Pecksniff's visage, as he pressed his hot hands together, and replied with humility, 'Quite disinterestedly. Sir, I assure you.'

'I know it,' said the Old Man, in his quiet way. 'I am sure of it. I said so. And that is why it will gratify you, and your two dear and equally disinterested daughters, to learn that your unselfish pleadings have prevailed. The—ahem! person whom I need not name, whom you know, for whom you so disinterestedly spoke, will

THE MEET AT ST. STEPHEN'S.

Gone to grass has he? Yes; but let nobody be surprised if the Grand Old Gee gallops up some fine morning as keen on the hunt as any of them.

—well, in point of fact, will, as you so ardently desire—*succeed to my fortune and inherit my estate !* '

Mr. Pecksniff's feelings and those of his daughters were too profound for words ; as the poet says of the thoughts aroused by the contemplation of a budding blossom— such as the primrose, perchance—those emotions lay ' too deep for tears.'

. . . .

Sincere sympathy for Sir William Harcourt, in being passed over as the successor to Mr. Gladstone for Premiership, was felt by both sides of the House. It was generally agreed that Lord Rosebery, brilliant and accomplished statesman as he is,

OLD MOTHER BUDGET (*née* TWITCHETT).

*Old Mother Budget she had but one eye
And a tail which she lost full speedily,*   *For every time she went through a division
She left a bit with the Opposition.*

could have waited for a future occasion to take the Premiership. Sir William could not. In his case it was—this year, two years, three years, never. Since the present Parliament will probably last over six years, it is never. Sir William's chances have been sacrificed by circumstances ; he might have been Lord Chancellor, it was his ambition, but he thought he would be Premier. Then, finding himself out of both, he would have been Speaker, but neither the time nor the turn of affairs allowed him to take that post. Now he finds himself left in Opposition with a diminished and dis- organised party to fight a long, weary battle against ' the strongest Government of the century.'

However, Sir William is gaining in popularity, and showing such excellent fighting powers that, probably, the public in general, and writers and caricaturists in particular, have hardly done him justice. Perhaps his pomposity has been the cause of a good deal of the banter. And then, his attitude to the late Government—whether real or manufactured one can hardly say—made him unpopular with those who saw in Lord Rosebery the failure of Mr. Gladstone as leader of the Liberal Party. Between these two gentlemen, the situation was amusingly reported to me, and tempted me at the time to illustrate two imaginary scenes, a fragment of which I here reproduce.

A CONVERSATION AT MALWOOD.

Scene: A country house in the New Forest; a study containing the usual furniture ; a table on which several volumes are carelessly laid, some open, some with book-marks between the leaves ; writing materials. *Time :* Sunday in the forenoon. Sir William Harcourt (*alone*). He turns over the volumes, makes extracts from them in a large commonplace book. Rises and walks about restlessly, his lips at intervals moving without any sound ; occasionally he bursts into broken words and sentences and into slight gestures, smiling at the same time complacently.

Sir W. H. : I had resolved to hold my tongue during the recess. Silence is gold, speech silver, and I am not a bimetallist. But those Derby people have insisted. One never knows when an extempore speech may not be forced on one at a few weeks' notice, and it is just as well to be prepared with one's improvisations.

[*He goes to the window. Observing some Sunday excursionists strolling apathetically about the grounds.*

Sir W. H. : Confound the fellows! I don't keep this place up for them. Do they take it for Chatsworth, and me for the Duke of Devonshire ? By all the laws of trespass, here's one of them got in !

[*A rather short and rotund person, in a loose coat and billycock hat, holding a belcher handkerchief to his face, enters mysteriously.*

Sir W. H. (*alarmea*): A dynamiter, by all that's explosive ! Where on earth is that detective ? (*With tremulous politeness*) If you have come upon—what shall I call it ?—an Irish errand, sir, you have made a slight mistake, though, of course, I am glad of anything which procures me the honour. I am not responsible for Irish affairs. You ought to see the Prime Minister. He lives in a large house in Berkeley Square, on the south side, in a courtyard : you can't mistake it.

'HERE'S A PRETTY HOWDAH DO!'

THE FIGURE (*disclosing himself*) : Why, Harcourt, don't you know me?

SIR W. H. (*to himself*) : Rosebery, by all that's puerile! Will he never have done with his schoolboy pranks? (*Aloud*) Why, of course I knew you. I thought I would have a little fun with you. But what's brought you here?

ROSEBERY : What of Mr. G.?

Sir W. H. : Well, he's all but gone. *Requiescat in pace.* But the combination of the learning of a German Professor with the habits of a middle-class financier leaves something lacking to the lettered statesman. Polite scholarship requires blood, noble at least, royal if possible, to give it the fine flavour, the delicate aroma of the time of Anne and the Georges. But come, shall we discuss our difficulties while we walk ? *Solvitur ambulando.* The peripatetic system of instruction suits me. If I were not afraid of boring you with family matters, I would take you to the stone that marks the place where our poor Rufus fell.

Rosebery : Well, that danger's gone. There are no bowmen here now. There are no tall deer.

Sir W. H. : There are no bowmen, but there may be dynamiters. I thought you were one. You really gave me a turn.

A CABINET COUNCIL, A FRAGMENT.

Harcourt : Well, are we all here ? Yes. No. Where is Rosey ? I forgot him. Confound the boy ! Why is he always late ? It is a quarter of an hour beyond the time named. Does anyone know where he is ?

Bryce : *Meettai saietahree Rosah quo locooroom sairah moraitoor.*

Harcourt : I must ask you, Bryce, to stop that unintelligible gibberish. It's worse than Mr. G.'s condensed versions. Hasn't Horace suffered enough from old Oxford, without being tortured by young Oxford, too ?

Bryce (*hurt*) : Well, all I know is, that is how Horahtious would have recited it himself.

Harcourt : Besides, *I* was going to say it. I object to have my quotations taken from me. I've got it down here. (*Produces a little memorandum-book.*)

Bryce (*sulkily, to John Morley*) : *L'esprit des autres.* (*Morley sniggers, and then looks supernaturally grave.*)

CAMPBELL-BANNERMAN : In the stable with his trainer, or at New Court with——

FOWLER (*mournfully*) : With his trainer, I very much fear.

HARCOURT : Well, we can do without him better than another.

Enter ROSEBERY, *hurried and breathless.*

HARCOURT (*continuing*) : Well, Rosey, where have you been ? In the stable with your trainer, or at New Court with— -eh ?

CAMPBELL-BANNERMAN (*aside*) : Oh !

HARCOURT : But I won't ask. *Mitte sectari Rosa quo locorum sera moretur*—Eh, Bryce ?

ROSEBERY : Upon my word, Harcourt, that is really very good, don't you know ? How you come to think of such things I really can't imagine.

HARCOURT (*complacently*) : A good classical education, Rosey. I did not leave the University without a degree, a fair memory, and a certain power of felicitous application. But really, Rosey, you're not up to date, you know. Ha, ha ! (*The Cabinet smiles collectively*) A quarter of an hour behind time ; and if punctuality, as I once told a certain illustrious personage, is the politeness of princes—he was much struck with the remark—it is a merit in a Minister. I speak both as a Plantagenet and as Chancellor of the Exchequer.

ROSEBERY : I am sure, Harcourt, I beg your pardon. I was nearly here—a good five minutes to spare, I assure you—when I suddenly remembered that I had forgotten something and went back for it. But when I got home I could not remember what it

was that I had forgotten, nor where I had put it, and, though I looked everywhere for it, I could not find it. (*To himself, seeing Harcourt consulting his note-book*) It was my book of impromptus and repartees—I can never face Harcourt without it.

Sir William is now practically leader of the Liberal Party, and, should his party come back to power in a reasonable time, he may yet have his ambition gratified. The elephantine work he has performed before, he may be ready to undertake again, but he must be cautious in not again being taken in by the wariness of the Irish Fox.

'*Sir William a fine figure. And Cromwellian too. Would look well in molten bronze.*'

(*With apologies to* BRITON RIVIERE, R.A.)

THE GOVERNMENT GEESE AND THE IRISH FOX.

Cackle: ' Home Rule is dead'; so now we can approach any Irish question without fear.

THE GAME OF GRAB.

WHEN the new Parliament met in 1895 it was soon seen that Mr. Joseph Chamberlain had played his game of Grab most successfully, by seeing that his Unionist friends had more than their share of the Parliamentary pie. No doubt Mr. Chamberlain had won the Parliamentary game by cleverness, and, naturally, the tricks were his. He had brought about the wonderful success of the combination Parliament by his balancing the two parties, the Unionists and the Conservatives, in his great St. Stephen's trick-act—who would have thought that—attended by the Primrose dame ; and, though Mr. Balfour was loudly cheered when he arrived in the newly made Parliament, and, although Mr. Chamberlain entered unnoticed, purely by accident (for he received quite an ovation when he rose to answer a question later), it was well felt in the House, as it was in the country, that Mr. Chamberlain was then, as he is now, the practical leader.

Mr. Joseph Chamberlain can with truth declare, 'Alone I did it' ; for the Conservative Party were afraid to put the country to the test, so Mr. Chamberlain took upon himself to show them the way, and the surprise he sprang upon the Government astonished the Tories quite as much as the Gladstonians. He simply told his little band of Unionists to sacrifice everything, to keep themselves in readiness, and to hold their tongues. They were not allowed to pair. And, when Mr. Brodrick, Member for Guildford, technically moved the reduction of the salary of the Secretary of War by one hundred pounds, no one suspected that this quiet little reduction of the salary of an independent and rich Minister was anything to disturb the equilibrium of Mr. Campbell-Bannerman. It was sure merely to gain a chance of quibbling over something to do with the reserve of small-arm ammunition. It was, however, anything but a small matter, for Mr. Brodrick's squib was sufficient to ignite the train of gunpowder laid by Mr. Chamberlain in readiness to blow up the Government. Bang went up one hundred pounds and a hundred votes.

Mr. Chamberlain, having won the first trick, was determined that his own partners should have the best cards, and in the game of Grab he got for his friends the lion's share of the sweets of office.

There is no doubt that Mr. Chamberlain is the most interesting figure in Parliament to - day. Few, if any, of our public men have had a more interesting career. He has practised in politics what theatrical managers have practised in plays—rehearsed and tried his performances in the country before bringing them to London. In Birmingham he played the same part, in a municipal way, he is now playing in Parliament in a national way, and with the same success.

THE MEETING OF PARLIAMENT: MR. BALFOUR ARRIVES.

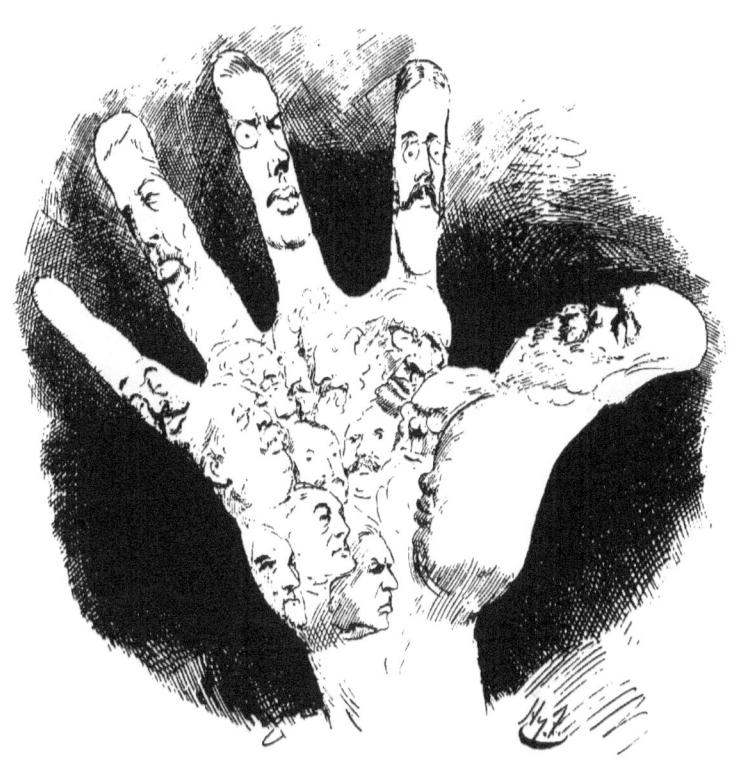

THE NEW PARLIAMENTARY HAND.

'JOEY'.

In his wonderful Balance Trick, to be seen nightly at the St. Stephen's Circus, Westminster.

THE NEW CABINET SEALS.

'YOUR LIFE OR YOUR SEAL!'

THE LION LYING DOWN WITH THE LAMB.

Mr. Chamberlain has managed to push himself up over Mr. Gladstone, then over the Duke of Devonshire, and now Lord Salisbury is merely his stepping-stone to a Peerage and the Premiership. His whole career can be summed up in one picture, 'The Seven Cham-Berlains of Brummagem.' Chamberlain the Republic at first—long dead. Left now to the vultures of the Press and the Caucus to screech over this fact when convenient to do so ; Chamberlain the Radical has been vanquished ; Chamberlain the Gladstonian has been left behind ; he then meets Chamberlain the Unionist, and is throwing him over as he meets Chamberlain the Tory. After that, as I said before, he meets Chamberlain the Peer.

Of course, Lord Salisbury is the most important figure in either House. He is the greatest Parliamentarian both to look at and to listen to, and is every inch a states-

MANY OLD FACES ARE MISSING.'

EXCELSIOR !

THE SEVEN CHAMBERLAINS OF BRUMMAGEM.

'THE KING OF THE MIDLANDS.'

THE NEW LEADER.

THERE WAS AN OLD WOMAN WHO
LIVED IN A SHOE.

man. Lord Salisbury's favourite attitude, when seated in the House, is half reclining, with his arms crossed, and head back, gazing up at the ornamental ceiling. He has a nervous peculiarity before rising to speak, or while listening to any of his colleagues in the House. When he is listening, or preparing to address the House himself, he sits, nervously moving his legs to and fro, even knocking them together, and never at rest for a second. So soon, however, as he rises, this irritability appears to quit him, and physically, as well as intellectually, the ideal statesman stands forth. Everyone must admit that Lord Salisbury's is an impressive figure, and that his deep, sonorous voice and majestic manner when speaking are highly attractive. He cannot resist his old love of satire, and sometimes he has a chance of showing that his powers of sarcasm are as trenchant as ever ; as, for instance, when Lord de Mauley rose to move 'That a Peer giving notice of his intention to offer his services to a constituency to represent them in the House of Commons shall be excused attendance in the House of Lords during the existence of that Parliament.' The burden of Lord de Mauley's lament seemed to be that it is a great misfortune to be born a Peer, and, when he pleaded for such ill-used individuals that they should be allowed to share in ' the rough and ready training afforded by the House of Commons,' the Premier characteristically observed that, if the noble Lord were inclined to offer his services to any constituency, there would be no danger of the House of Lords inflicting any penalty upon him for absenting himself from the deliberations of that House. At this the Upper House laughed consumedly, and it would be rather interesting to know to how many Members of the Hereditary Chamber Lord Salisbury could have correctly replied in the same terms.

Now that Lord Rosebery was out of office, and the House of Lords was safe from attack for years to come, Lord Salisbury and others could well indulge to their hearts' content in humorous allusions to the question.

The Opposition, on the other hand, were extremely touchy. They were making mountains out of mole-hills. The Honourable Campbell-Bannerman, who had lost the Speakership in exchange for a very limited period in office, waxed very wroth about the delivering up of the Seals of Office. The affable Minister became the irritable outsider ; and, when Lord Rosebery retired and told the Opposition that they might keep Downing Street in order and become the responsible servants of John Bull, there was a funny little incident about the keys. Lord Salisbury, in a practical, unsentimental way, sent his aide-de-camp Schomberg McDonnell to ask for them, and, meeting Mr. Campbell-Bannerman, he asked that gentleman whether he had such a thing about him as a seal with a key attached. This was afterwards described by Lord Rosebery in the House of Lords in such a tragic way that one pictures the Honourable Schomberg McDonnell as a veritable highwayman, demanding from the unfortunate ex-Minister

OUT OF HIS DEPTH.

'Lord Salisbury has been led to adopt a very erroneous view of the character of the report of the London Amalgamation Commissioners.'—*The Times.*

' his life or his seal ' ; taking us back to the days of Dick Turpin or Claude Duval.

The Seals in the Cabinet tank I here present. (Page 125.)

The new Government came in like a lamb, lying down with the lion. For nothing could have been more beautiful than the sympathetic regard the leader of the Opposition, Sir William Harcourt, showed to the leader of the Government, the lamb-like Mr. Balfour. Perhaps he felt released from the

MR. C. T. RITCHIE FINDING A SEAT AT LAST.

MOTHER RITCHIE AND HER CHILD.

hardness of Parliamentary strife by the absence of many Members who acted as *picadors* in rousing to attack his opponents.

Mr. Conybeare, Mr. Keir Hardie, Mr. Cleophas Morton, Mr. Cremer, Mr. Caine, and other disturbing elements, were left in the cold outside Parliament, so peace for the time reigned within.

LORD HIGH TURNCOCK.

A TANNER ON THE RAMPAGE.

Sir William at first, strange to say, found himself outside of the leadership of the Opposition ; Mr. Timothy Healy arrogated to himself that post. He positively took the lead of the business of the House for the Opposition, and, when Sir William rose to speak, it was only on the authority of Mr. Healy. Mr. Healy was the substance, Sir William merely the shadow of authority. But the Commons was really Mr. Chamberlain's, he had made it his own. The King of the Midlands had become the King of the Ministers. Lord Salisbury rushed madly in where angels like Mr. Chamberlain feared to tread. Mr. Chamberlain, for instance, would never have made the mistake Lord Salisbury did over the London Government problem a year before ; nor would he, I imagine, have burdened himself with that army of little Bills which placed him in the position of the old woman who lived in her shoe, who had so many children.

In the new Parliament the return of Mr. Ritchie to office was looked upon as a strong element in what was considered already a strong Government. He had been wasting his time whipping that bumptious child of his, the London County Council, into good behaviour ; but now he finds metal more attractive in attending to work in his old seat in Parliament.

Mr. Chaplin was also welcomed back in the Government at last, as President of the Local Government Board, and, when the dog days came, he had to act as Lord High Turncock in relief of distressed East-enders in their hour of need, owing to the water famine.

By the way, it was in August that the Irish party were carrying on their own little Parliament in Committee Room 15, a room about which a well-known Parliamentary writer remarks, ' They uncrowned their king

PRIVATE SATISFACTION.

THE IRISH BABBLE SHOP: COMMITTEE ROOM NO. 15.

once upon a time, and brought in a potentate, named Chaos, to rule in his stead.' If Mr. Chamberlain had that Kodak referred to a few pages back, his view of Room No. 15 would be something like what is shown on page 137. And I may here note the fact that it was at this very time that Dr. Tanner came down from Room No. 15 on the rampage. It was the scene in which Dr. Tanner, when he was turned out of the House, roared at Mr. Chamberlain the well-remembered 'Judas, Judas, Judas!'

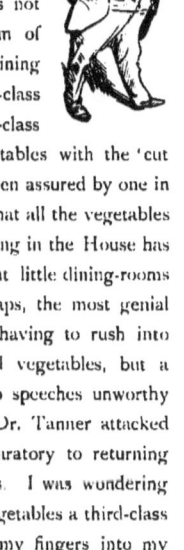

I recollect another incident which happened, worth recording as typical of the volatile Doctor.

The fact came out once in 'Supply,' that Dr. Tanner was not satisfied with the vegetables supplied to him in the dining-room of the House of Commons. He informed the House that the dining arrangements were worse than were to be found in any third-class restaurant in the City. I have not any experience of third-class restaurants, but I doubt very much whether they give three vegetables with the 'cut off the joint,' as they do in the House of Commons ; and I have been assured by one in authority that no exception is made in Dr. Tanner's case, and that all the vegetables are supplied to him without reserve. In spite of Dr. Tanner, dining in the House has never been so popular as it has been of late years. The pleasant little dining-rooms hard by the Terrace have been well patronised, and provide, perhaps, the most genial gatherings of the London season—marred merely by Members having to rush into the House for endless divisions, to return to not only cold vegetables, but a cold dinner, and sometimes to remain in the House to listen to speeches unworthy of a third-class debating forum. I recollect the very evening Dr. Tanner attacked the cuisine ; I was putting on my gloves in the Lobby, preparatory to returning home, when Dr. Tanner brushed past me from the dining-rooms. I was wondering how many vegetables he had had for dinner, and what style of vegetables a third-class restaurant-keeper would give a customer, and had just slipped my fingers into my second glove, when some 'high words' reached me from the inner Chamber. I rushed into the House and was nearly knocked over by these words, 'The right hon. gentleman is one of the basest and meanest skunks that ever sat upon the bench !' And this from Dr. Tanner, because (to use Dr. Tanner's own expression) the Home Secretary had called him a 'vulgarian.' Now, had Mr. Matthews called him a 'vegetarian,' probably the result would have been even worse. But for Mr. Sexton, there is no doubt Dr. Tanner would have been 'named.' The scene that followed would have given the frequenters of a third-class City restaurant an interesting and edifying sample of the manners and customs of the 'best club in England.'

Dr. Tanner remained, 'looking daggers,' and said something about the New

Scotland Yard buildings being 'a vulgar interruption.' This was directed to the Home Secretary, but the House was too dull quite to see the point, and it is too late in the day now to explain it.'

Another peculiar and eccentric, but more genial Member of the Irish Party is Mr. William Field, who once at question time asked Mr. Campbell-Bannerman to give him 'private satisfaction.' The House at the moment was thrilled, its memory went back to the days of duelling and bloodthirsty combats, whilst, after all, Mr. Field really meant to have said 'private information.' In the good old days, with the good old stock of Irish Members, they acted differently.

For instance, the O'Gorman Mahon, who was the Grand Old Man of the Irish Party, was a fine, handsome, picturesque old gentleman, with grey hair, moustache, and beard, a splendid type of the fine old gentleman of the fighting school. He had fought some duels in his day, and, as he wandered about the Lobby and growled at injustice to 'Oireland,' he seemed in his thoughts to be fighting them over again. And, curious to relate, it is on record that Mr. Gladstone once referred to his skill as a duellist, with unfeigned and unqualified admiration. Except as a picturesque figure, he attracted very little attention during the time of which I am writing. He walked with the rest of his party wearily through the Division Lobbies.

Major O'Gorman I have but a slight recollection of, although once seen he could never be forgotten. He made up in bulk what the O'Gorman Mahon held in picturesqueness, and it may be said of the Major that, when he departed, he left a big gap in the benches upon which he was accustomed to roll, and from which his sonorous voice would go forth and resound through the furthermost corners of the House. He was another of the good 'ould bhoys' who threw orthodox rules and manners to the winds, and he was a chartered humorist in the House, polishing off a whole joint and a whole bottle, whilst the more delicate Saxon would be content with his cutlet, and small whisky and seltzer.

Another popular Member that I must include among the good old Irish Members is Sir Patrick O'Brien, always popular, always ready. As a proof of his humour, I recall an incident on a late sitting of the House in March 1885, one of the nights of obstruction. Mr. T. P. O'Connor, who was the Obstructionist at the time, was making one of his rather long speeches, when Sir Patrick O'Brien, getting tired of it, began to chatter to those around him. The House was nearly empty at the moment, I need hardly say, so that 'Tay Pay' could not but notice the interruptions, and he appealed against the irritating behaviour of his fellow countryman; when Sir Patrick O'Brien retorted, 'The hon. gentleman misinterprets my motive; I interrupted, it is true, but it was with the intention of waking the hon. gentleman's audience.' Sir Patrick, I may add, was one of the inner circle of good fellows who met in Captain Gosset's room.

'ALL THAT WAS LEFT OF THEM.'

FAIRGAME certainly are Working-men Politicians. They are a very different class from the working men themselves. All must admire the horny-handed son of toil, and the typical honest British workman ; but these gentlemen —I use the word advisedly—who represent their fellows in Parliament are, with very few exceptions, working the men rather than working men.

What is a working man ? Professor Bryce, the great authority on the Government of Republican America, was asked this simple question in reference to the

THE GATESHEAD GIANT.

A genuine Working Man.

innovation of putting working men in the place of county gentlemen on the borough benches. The Professor confirmed Mr. Chamberlain's description of the last Gladstonian Government—'a deaf and dumb institution'—by being speechless. The poor City clerk, who *does* work ten hours a day for a pound a week, is not a working man; but the able-bodied artisan, who refuses to work nine hours for twice that amount, is. The jaded artist, who toils in his studio from sunrise to sunset, painting pot-boilers to support his wife and family, is not a working man; but the house decorator, who is painting his door outside, adjourning between each daub to the public-house round the corner, and who walks home at five o'clock, is. The Doctor, who is attending his patients morning, noon, and night, is not a working man; but the idle loafer, who breaks heads up his alley for the overtaxed medical man to mend, is. The curate, who is at his duties for twenty hours out of the twenty-four, for the merest pittance, is not a working man; but the labourer who digs a grave once a month, and is drinking himself into his own meanwhile, is. The labourer is the spoilt pet of the

Parliamentarian. Professor Bryce, although he failed to define what a working man is, when in authority, made Magistrates of working men wholesale ; but, in putting them on the bench, he must have been aware that, if a man has time to be a Magistrate, instead of earning his bread, he can no longer be a working man. Sending the working man to Parliament is, in the opinion of many, a mistake. Certainly he is not a success as a legislator. Mr. Burt is supposed to be the brilliant exception, but, is he exactly brilliant ? Does not his success lie in the fact that, unlike the other working men, he is modest, sincere, and silent ; in fact, as unlike the typical working man M.P. as possible?

Mr. Broadhurst is a stolid, able son of toil at one time translated into a Minister. It was he who, when in the Government, protested against the Court dress at the Speaker's Levée, and broke down that old tradition of special costume for the hand-shaking function. It may be mentioned that not only the Speaker pacified the wearers of fustian, but Royalty also. His Royal Highness the Prince of Wales follows the example set him by his father in paying all possible respect to the masses. Those who have read Lord Shaftesbury's interesting 'Memoirs,' will recollect a significant passage relating to the Prince Consort's visit to the East-end

PUSSY CAT, PUSSY CAT.
(MR. KEIR HARDIE, M.P.)

'*Pussy cat, pussy cat, where have you been ?*'
'*I've been to St. Stephen's to sneer at the Queen.*'
'*Pussy cat, pussy cat, what did you there ?*'
'*I'm afraid I got snubbed by the House and the Chair.*'

of London, which visit would have never been made but for Lord Shaftesbury's insisting upon it. The Prince, finding it so greatly augmented his popularity, probably passed the hint on to his son. This, and the fact that he is Member for North-East Norfolk, where the Sandringham estate is situated, is most likely the cause of Joseph Arch's being so petted by Royalty. He is invited to Royal functions whenever there is a chance, and on one occasion he waxed very wroth when he was not allowed into the Imperial Institute conversazione because he was not in evening dress. Indignantly he informed the door-keepers that he would tell His Royal Highness. This threat had the desired effect, and Mr. Arch was allowed into the building attired in fustian. ' The people's Arch ' once received an invitation to the Queen's garden party, and noting ' Morning dress' upon the card, nothing would convince the Member for North-East Norfolk that this was not done by Her Majesty for his especial benefit ; ' for surely,' said he, ' they wear evening dress for a garden party at night time !'   How very considerate of Her Majesty !   However, a paragraph was sent the round of the papers to say that Mr. Arch had a political engagement, and could not therefore grace the occasion.

Mr. Arch looks the labourer, but never the M.P.   He rubs his hands up and down his coat while he speaks and previous to shaking hands, and is still ready with a rough epigram, which may be all right for the ' horny-handed son of toil ' at election time in Norfolk, but rather grates upon the weary, go-as-you-please legislators still left in the ' best club ' at St. Stephen's.

The worst of the working man representative is that he soon becomes the idle M.P.   The first signs of the change are apt to be a patronising attitude to his own party, and a habit of ridiculing them to others.   For instance, I heard, the first year I attended Parliament, the then representative of the working man, Mr. McDonald, snub in a most arrogant manner a Working Man's Committee he was interviewing. ' We gentlemen here can't be worried by the likes o' you, you know ; ' and I noted that the little deputation, while they said nothing, walked off highly offended.   Naturally this kind of thing opens working men's eyes to the fact that the Labour Member is a very different man inside the House from what he is outside ; and the fact that at the last election the labour candidates were all but excluded shows that their constituents have but little faith in them.   Though the House is very indulgent indeed, it is tickled at times with the *H-less* harangues of the working man's representative.   I remember one such Member who, unfortunately, had to introduce the Eels Bill.   He did so in the following words :—

' Hi 'ave the honour to hintroduce to this 'ouse this hevening the Heels Bill, which 'as just been haccepted by the Hupper 'ouse.'

And I must confess that the House on this occasion burst out laughing.   The returns to Parliament of the working men were few and far between, until Mr. John Burns, Mr. Keir Hardie, and others were returned *en masse*, and the Labour Party seemed, at last, as if it would be a party to reckon with ; but it has since practically disappeared.   Mr. Keir Hardie, who made his entry into the House in the manner of a circus proprietor entering a village, got his reputation there by wearing a brown deer-stalker hat ; and, when he discarded this for a time for a black one, the papers chronicled the event with the minuteness they would have devoted to any important change in the Royal family, or in the Government of the country ; and, if he were now in Parliament, and would change this hat for a Tam o' Shanter, and then adopt a Glengarry, he would keep his name before the public.   Such is notoriety !

OUTSIDE THE HOUSE.

'HONEST' TOM TIMESERVER (loq.): 'Wot does Members o' Parly-ment do for yer? W'y, nuffink! They lounges in heavy chairs, mops up champagne, and keeps their mouths shut with a fust-class cigar and a little chapse. Yuss! feller-workmen, and hexpecks us to black their boots and kiss their feet! That's what I cort's 'UMBUG!!'

INSIDE THE HOUSE.

'HONEST' TOM TIMESERVER (loq.): 'I tell yer wot, honourable Ministers, the British workman's a 'umbug! You jest leave 'im ter me an' I'll see that 'e 'olds 'is rowe an' gives yon 'is wotes, my noble pals!'

AN ELECTION EXTRAVAGANZA.

BY A CRUSTED TORY.

'BEGGARS' IN DOWNING STREET.

'If the Cabinet shirk the question, they will, in plain English, throw away the Labour vote, and compromise the future of the party.' Daily Chronicle.

BURNS 'DIMINUENDO.'

At the Dock Gates.   *In Hyde Park.*   *In Parliament.*

In 1893 there were two or three questions about the payment of Members, and once or twice the proposal kept the attention of the House for quite an important time, when it was only 'brought out for an airing,' but none of the big boys on the Conservative side threw stones at it. The little subject might some day become a big one, which would be for the benefit of either party to favour, so both the front benches wisely avoided the question. On one occasion when the subject was paraded, it was left to the good-natured Admiral Field to chaff it, but the serious opposition was postponed until it was brought up again, when, to the astonishment of all, Mr. Gladstone threw cold water upon it. It was generally expected he would have done the reverse, and the working expectant Members were horribly chagrined by the Premier's (for he was leader at the time) ignoring their request. He had metal more attractive at the time that lured all his affections away from any pet subject but Home

Rule. At this time there happened to be some all-night sittings, and it struck some that, if Members were to be paid, we should very soon have the Eight Hours' movement adopted in the House, and avoid the weary, long, wasted hours. Not that the payment system guarantees that there shall be no more waste of time, for I have seen 'filibustering' in Congress delay business just as much as obstruction in the Commons.

If Parliament is to be run on this purely commercial basis, why not be consistent —pay the players and charge the public for admission? Why not make Parliament self-supporting? Fancy the houses that would be realised! Seats would be at a premium on occasions such as that on which Mr. Gladstone introduced his Home Rule Bill, and the booking would always be good whenever a scene was anticipated. Outside St. Stephen's Hall behold placards—'Speaker's Gallery Full!' 'Strangers' Gallery Full!' 'Ladies' Gallery, Standing Room Only!' 'Box office open in Westminster Hall—hours 10 to 5.' Then would the lot of the M.P. be muchly ameliorated.

Lord Rosebery's Cabinet shirked the question of paying Members, which made these gentlemen and their paper, the 'Daily Chronicle,' very angry, as is shown in my cartoon reproduced on page 147.

Mr. John Burns came to the House with a more solid reputation. He had made himself notorious in the Coal Strike, and had become a Member of the London County Council. Besides, he had the good fortune to be called 'John.' It is curious that *John* seems to have an advantage over most other Christian names in politics. *John* Morley and *John* Dillon have been known as honest John Morley, honest John Dillon, then came John Burns, and of course he must be 'honest' John Burns.

Burns played his political cards better than Keir Hardie when he first went into the House. The wearer of the deer-stalker cap came to grief sadly in essaying to move the adjournment of the House, and he attempted other Parliamentary manœuvres in which he was a 'prentice hand; he only made himself ridiculous. Keir Hardie's face has not the strength of Burns', and that index to the character, the eye, denotes that the volatile Scotchman has neither the ability nor the stability of the Member for Battersea. Yet, up to the present, Burns has done nothing whatever in the House to add to the reputation he made outside the House. Sometimes one thinks Mr. John Burns is likely to develop into a mere *farceur*, instead of deserving that 'honest John'—a *sobriquet* which, as I have already stated, is beginning to savour of clap-trap. Mr. John Burns is in the habit of making jokes, but he does not always inform his hearers that what he says is meant for humour. His appearance on a Music Hall stage one Sunday evening was anything but imposing, and I doubt whether, if he 'opened' at an ordinary Music Hall on an ordinary evening, the paying public would sit quietly and listen to his choice wit, as displayed in his tirade against the House of Lords, which he calls the 'guilty Chamber.' His humorous remark to the effect that the Queen and the Prince of Wales should 'take the Lords by the scruff of the neck and kick them out,' is worth putting on record as a sample of the taste of the Member for Battersea. This kind of thing may go down in that constituency, or even at a Music Hall in London in the West-end on a Sunday evening, but it is impossible in the House of Commons; and, as Mr. Burns soon discovered, will not be tolerated on the other side of the Atlantic.

When Greek meets Greek then comes the tug of war. Probably such an exchange of abuse as took place in the autumn of 1894, at the Labour Conference, when all these exalted working men took off the gloves, was never heard before. The following lines, sent to me at the time, are well worth quoting :—

THE DIGNITY OF LABOUR.

A.—Comrade in the sacred cause,
    Let us stretch our brazen jaws,
    And, to right imagined wrong,
    Chant an acrimonious song.
    But (observe this horny fist !)
    I must be the soloist.

B.—Brother in the strife with law,
    I am with you jaw to jaw.
    If you want a stirring song,
    I'm the man to pitch it strong.
    Hence on this I must insist :
    I shall be the soloist.

A.—Brother in the cause of Labour,
    No one should defame his neighbour.
    Vulgar personal abuse
    Will admit of no excuse.
    Yet I'm driven to pronounce
    You a bounder on the bounce.

B.—Bounding brother, boom away :
    Every ass must have his bray.

Personalities, I own,
Lower Labour's moral tone.

Yet, since truth must be confest,
' Bullying boss ' describes you best.

A.—Brazen, bullyragging boozer,
    Blatant Boanerges—you, Sir !
B.—Bold, bombastic, bumptious bruiser,
    Bellowing bull of Bashan—*you*, Sir !
Both.—Brothers in the cause of Labour
    Never vilify their neighbour.

If Mr. Burns will take friendly advice, and really wishes to succeed in Parliament, as have other representatives of working men, let him remember that everyone finds his level in the House of Commons. Let him beware lest he fall, as others have, by forgetting the virtue of modesty, and that his strength lies in being still one of the people. If not, it will be :—

HUMPTY DUMPTY.

The Member for Battersea.

Humpty dumpty sat on a wall,
Humpty Dumpty had a great fall,
And neither King Demos, nor true working men
Could make him a Radical zealot again.

JOHN AND JONATHAN.

[Apropos of the visit of Mr. John Burns, M.P., to the United States.]

PERHAPS no Member of the Best Club in recent years has caused such a surprising stir as Jabez Spencer Balfour—a commonplace little dumpling of a man. When he flitted about the House, I could not resist the temptation of caricaturing him, but his sympathies, when in Parliament, were merely with his guinea-pigs; politically he was a cipher.

I used to sketch him for 'Punch,' as I saw him either running into the House, or more often sitting on the benches with his little legs hanging over the sides, fast asleep all the time. He looked the picture of charming simplicity. It is like speaking of a mummy to bring Jabez Balfour to the front again. He is now out of sight and out of mind for some time, and I do not suppose that he ever will again be the sensation of the hour.

I see him now, as I saw him then in the House, childlike and bland, in his seat in the House of Commons, the puritanical financier, sleeping the sleep of the innocent babe. Below are some lines written on Jabez thirty years ago by his admiring friend, the Rev. Dawson Burns, D.D. :—

> I saw thee when a new-born babe,
>   A stranger come to town ;
> And size and form both seem to say
>   He's destined for renown.
> And now what shall I wish for thee,
>   All good in heart and mind,
> A joy to all thy friends and thee,
>   A blessing to mankind.

Poets were always prophets.

THE INFANT JABEZ. (*With apologies to* G. F. WATTS, R.A.)

'What's in a name?' Well, a great deal when any one bearing the same cognomen as yourself degrades it, and the stupid British public, or a portion of it, is incapable of defining between the pure and the base metal. The name of J. S. Balfour has been daily before us for some years in connection with the investigations into gigantic swindling operations going on in London, whilst Jabez Balfour was enjoying himself in luxury and growing his orchids out of reach of the law. So also was the name of A. J. Balfour daily before us during the Irish debate, as the name of the

JABEZ AS BO-PEEP.

Leader of the Opposition, and as an authority outside the House on bi-metallism and golf. Yet—would you credit it?—there were people asinine enough to imagine that the Right Hon.

The Bold Bowles as a Popular Privateer

A. J. and the runaway Jabez were one and the same person! I was riding past the lower part of Hampstead Heath about that time and overheard a political agitator holding forth under a tree, and denouncing to the public the Leader of the Opposition, and loudly proclaiming that his patronymic was one 'as stinks in hour nostrils!' 'Yas,' said one of his audience, 'the cove what sprung the Liberator Company!' 'A fair 'ave, that wos,' said another, 'Salisbury's pal, and the people's henemy!' and so on. I wished some one had cut out the sketch, which I published at the time in my London Letter, and pasted it upon the agitators' tree at 'Ampstead, and other places, just to show the difference between the Right Honourable A. J. Balfour and Jabez Balfour the dis——

So soon as Mr. Jabez Balfour discovered he was a marked man, he moved too rapidly and too far

Crier Cremer: 'Oyez! Oyez! Oyez! Wanted, a runaway Skipper, and the people who helped him to skip!'

FAUST UP TO DATE.

MARGUERITE . LORD KIMBERLEY.
THE ROSE . JABEZ.

MARGUERITE. '*He comes, he cometh not.*'

WELCOME, LITTLE STRANGER!

*How pleased all good men will be if Jabez really spends his Christmas
in his native land!*

afield to suit the authorities, and he was soon 'wanted' by the police.   His
portrait, I have seen stated, is in the 'Hue and Cry.'   This journal, with its cuts
of and chats about criminals, is not published in this country, but is an Irish
periodical.   The 'Police Gazette' is the more dignified title of the organ of our modern
'Bow Street Runners.'   Curiosity compelled me to glance through the copy containing
a portrait of Mr. Spencer Balfour, and all I can say is that that gentleman, wherever
he may be, might have lived in the utmost peace and immunity if his detection had
depended solely upon the likeness published in the 'Gazette.'   Now, why, in a serious
matter like this, do the police depend solely upon a bad engraving from a bad photograph?   I once illustrated how a Member of Parliament could disguise his face, but it
is impossible for any one effectually to disguise his figure.   It is important that the

AT LAST !

The Argentine Republic delivers Jabez to England.

figure of any one ' wanted ' should be known, so I show here a silhouette of the missing director. As a matter of fact, I haven't seen a single portrait of this gentleman in any periodical that resembles him in the least. Indeed, it was not until Balfour was at last brought back, that any portraits appeared of him that were a bit like the original.

The extraordinary career of this Member of Parliament will surely stand unique in the annals of Parliament for a long time to come. There was a little extra sensation during Balfour's absence, for many thought his return would implicate other Members of Parliament who had, without knowing the true nature of their fellow Member, undertaken directorships and other offices at his instigation ; and the Nonconformist conscience was sadly worried at that momentous time, and, when Parliament met in 1895, the topic of conversation was the absent Jabez.

Detectives went, and detectives came back, but Jabez remained. Some, in fact, thought the money strings that enabled him to evade justice were pulled by those on this side. Mr. Cremer, who was then in Parliament, became crier, and spoke of ' some singular rumours afloat ' on this point ; that money had been sent to the exile of Salta, 'for the ostensible purpose of assisting in making of water works,' whilst the Government itself had spent over 6,400*l.* in lawyers' bills and detectives' expenses without any result. Bold ' Tommy ' Bowles offered to bring him back himself, and in his speech in the House expressed contempt for those sea-dogs who had failed to bring the prisoner across the water. Lord Kimberley, at the Foreign Office, was much troubled by the continued heckling anent the missing Jabez, and in the Foreign Office version of 'Faust,' Lord Kimberley is depicted at the time as Marguerite, exclaiming, as he tears the petals of the rose, ' He comes, he cometh not ; he comes, he cometh not !'

At last, the Argentine Republic dropped the ex-Member of the English Parliament into the hands of Justice. The little Republic was glad to get rid of the little rogue—after she had got all the money she could out of him. I was one of those present in Bow Street on the morning Jabez Balfour was brought into the dock. By that time the public were weary of him, and there was really very little interest in the proceedings, particularly since it was then known that those who had felt unsafe during his absence were now assured that they would not be worried.

Perhaps it is not out of place for me here to introduce a few of the sketches I made in Bow Street of the ex-Member of Parliament, one of the most extraordinary personalities that ever deceived his friends and the public.

The mention of Jabez Balfour naturally suggests the treadmill. Parliament is a treadmill. The poor Ministers have to tread away, hour after hour, day after day, that

M

NOTING POINTS.

CONSULTING HIS SOLICITOR.

TAKING NOTES.

JABEZ BALFOUR: A SKETCH IN COURT.

IN THE DOCK.

THE PARLIAMENTARY TREADMILL.

mill of Parliamentary work that goes round and round and round, and results in very little.

When the Estimates have been discussed, the poor Minister has to meet the heckling of the faddists, that little band of Members who take the greatest delight in quibbling over small matters, enjoying their joke at the expense of a Minister, from whom they expect information on everything, from the ventilators and the wash-house at a Royal Palace, to the latest burners used on the staircase of the House of Commons. Mr. Labouchere plays the leading part among those who cavil at petty disbursements in connection with the Royal palaces and parks, and, sometimes, he is most entertaining in his dissertations on such matters; but generally the House is empty, and it is left to a few Members, and the Speaker and officials of the House, to enjoy the witticisms emanating from the honourable Member on such occasions. I recollect once, when Mr. Labouchere was playing in his old *rôle* of the general quibbler, the House was so empty that a journalistic friend of mine (need I say that he was Scotch?) was led to make a rather apposite comparison between the empty Chamber, in which stood one solitary figure declaiming to long rows of empty benches, and one of Mr. Orchardson's pictures. Mr. Plunket, now Lord Rathmore, referred to elsewhere, was the best possible Member of the Government to bear the quips and cranks in which Mr. Labouchere, Sir George Campbell, Mr. Morton, and a few other aggressive spirits chose to indulge. But it required all his gifts of graceful expression to frame pacific replies in answer to the long string of stale and reiterated complaints. It was quite pathetic to hear Sir George Campbell declare that he had often passed Holyrood Palace, but had never gone in, because, although he was a Scotchman at heart, there was sixpence to pay. He said that, as a taxpayer, he begrudged parting with this little coin, and rather anxiously pleaded that, although it was levied by the base Saxon, yet Americans and other foreigners who go to see the Palace, without understanding the financial arrangements of this country, set it down to the credit of his countrymen, and depart swearing roundly 'at those stingy Scotch!'

But the emptiness of the House when the Estimates are on (which I have alluded to here) is an old Parliamentary joke. The man on the hustings seeking to be a Member declares that, once in Parliament, he will pay all attention to the burning question of Expenditure; when he gets in, he takes a holiday when such dull matters are before the House. Mr. Chamberlain spoke very bitterly on this point once, when the question was up about the importation of prison-made goods, and regretted he had not a Kodak picture of the House to send to the constituencies of the people's representatives who spoke so loudly on platforms on matters of this kind. However, there are a few exceptions to the general rule of Members. Admiral Field, the Member for Eastbourne, for instance, is always on the watch, and, like the good old sea-dog he is, is ready to pilot any question concerning the Navy through the House, whether he has an audience or not.

Mr. Courtney, since he left the Chairmanship of the House, is ready to lecture the Committee, even if the Committee is represented by one gentleman only on the Government bench; and Mr. Pickersgill is ever flitting about the doors, and is disconsolate, should there not be something connected with greater London to pounce upon.

If there are matters concerning the kitchen, instead of prison-made goods, there is sure to be a little more interest, and I well recollect how Mr. Sidney Herbert, before

'KODAK'-ING THE COMMONS.

' I am afraid it would be out of order to "Kodak" the House of Commons at any time, but I wish we could have a photograph of the House of Commons during this discussion and send it by the million throughout the constituencies, that they might see the interest which some of the people's representatives take in questions on which they speak very loudly on platforms.'— From Mr. Chamberlain's speech in the House against the importation of prison-made goods. Tuesday, February 19.

*The old Sea-Dog awakening. 'Sheet anchor! where?
All hands to the pumps!'*

The tailor does not make the M.P.

he became Earl of Pembroke, appeared in the character of a fascinating steward, to give a faithful account of his stewardship to the House about the expenses of the Kitchen Committee.

MR. PICKERSGILL DISCON-
SOLATE.

Talking of prison-made goods, I recollect a very funny article's appearing in a serious publication devoted to the tailoring trade, about the atrocious costumes worn by Members in our House of Commons. The writer wondered whether some philanthropic Members did not really have prison-made clothes! And a friend of mine wrote some doggerel *à propos* of an expression in that article referring to one Member in particular, that 'his trousers are rather baggy at the knees.'

Mr. Sidney Herbert, Caterer-in-Chief, pondering over the Kitchen Committee Balance Sheet.

FASHIONS IN THE HOUSE.

'*Rather baggy at the knees.*'

With flashing eye and outstretch'd hand
The Statesman holds the House in spell.
His eloquence, in truth, is grand ;
' Hear, hear !'—loud cheers—he does it well.
But in the gallery on high
A stranger, sneering, disagrees,
And hisses, ' Look !—his trousers—why
They're " rather baggy at the knees."'

The victory's won ; the Bill is passed ;
The Statesman stands exhausted now.
Upon his head the incense cast—
The laurel wreath upon his brow !
Nay ; something here our mem'ry jogs
Which makes our ardour chill and freeze—
We notice that his nether togs
Are ' rather baggy at the knees !'

A DREAM OF FAIR WOMEN IN THE LADIES' GALLERY.

AFTER A 'SCENE' IN THE
LADIES' GALLERY.

ERILY, the most difficult problem the officials of the
House have to deal with at present is that relating to
the admission of ladies. Years ago their visits were few
and far between ; it was only on an exceptional night
that the Ladies' Gallery would be full. Perhaps I am
personally to blame for the change, if I am to credit
what the officials tell me, that after I travelled through
the country on tour, giving my ' Humours of Parliament,'
in which I show pictures of ladies in the House, and
the pleasant little tea parties on the Terrace, the country
cousins then flocked to the House in numbers.

One of the most notable features of the last session
or two has been the number of ladies who besiege the
House of Commons ; the Terrace, the dining-rooms, the

TRIUMPH !

lobbies, and even parts of the House itself ; and, although some old Parliamentary hands refuse to receive them, and set their faces against the charmers' intrusion, the majority seem glad to pass the weary days in the pleasant company of their fair friends. When the end of the Home Rule question drew near, the ladies took the House by storm in a different way. They were not seeking tea on the Terrace, or dinner, or even a seat to hear the debate ; they wished to have a voice in the great question before Parliament, and to present to Her Majesty a petition against Home Rule, signed by upwards of 100,000 Irishwomen. They wished to present it themselves, but Mr. Asquith, the Home Secretary, refused to receive them. How ungallant ! And how injudicious ; for though ladies have no votes themselves, they influence many ; and now the Home Secretary has given offence to ladies in general, which probably jeopardised the chances of his party at the election. Such a mistake would never have happened had Mr. Woodall been Home Secretary ; and, moreover, just fancy the picture of Sir Richard Temple presenting such a charming petition to Her Majesty, personally conducting the fair representatives with that gallantry peculiarly his own ! The Home

Secretary ought to be made to stand on the steps of St. Stephen's Great Hall and read out the 100,000 names, as a just penance for his want of courtesy. Alas! Sir Richard Temple no longer flits cupid-like about the House, or has his beauty sleep on the benches.

A few years ago the ladies politically inclined had quite a thrill of excitement when the Parish Councils Woman Suffrage Bill passed by a majority of 21, and there was a serious motion to abolish the 'grill,' that is, the screen in front of the Ladies' Gallery.

SIR RICHARD'S DREAM OF FAIR WOMEN.

'THE OPPOSITION ENDS IN SMOKE.' By a Radical Artist.

The LAST SESSION

 SOME strong, healthy, vigorous man has said that the only use in having a good constitution is the pleasure one has in ruining it; and it may be said of the present Government that the only pleasure they had in coming into power with phenomenal majority was in the pains they have taken since to reduce it.

Certainly last Session 'the strongest Government of our time' very nearly proved itself one of the weakest—that is, in connection with home policy. Its foreign policy no one, except the 'Daily Chronicle,' perhaps, can find fault with; and, after all, England's foreign policy should be 99 per cent. of the work of any Cabinet of this country.

The sketches in this chapter were printed in the 'Daily News,' and are republished by permission. They were naturally drawn in an open style to suit rapid newspaper printing, and are perhaps interesting from the fact that they were actually drawn in the Press gallery of the House during the debates, and sent from the gallery to the engravers, not afterwards being improved upon or touched. These are probably the only Parliamentary sketches ever made direct in pen-and-ink in the House during a sitting and printed a few hours after being drawn from life.

Domestic subjects get far too much attention in some Governments. I think it was Mr. Joseph Cowan who drew a picture of domestic policy as compared with foreign policy. He said that, if you heard a servant fall downstairs and break a trayful of crockery, you would shrug your shoulders and say, ' Well, we must have this replaced '

—that is domestic policy. But if there was a row in the street, and your house was in jeopardy, you would send for the biggest policeman to protect you—that is foreign policy. Now, England has not only a row on one side of her house, but she has it all around. Every street has gangs of people shouting to attack her, and even the alleys are infected, and who knows but underground mines are not endangering the safety of

THE CRY IS STILL—THEY GO!

her house? It is therefore a good thing that Lord Salisbury—for surely he is the big policeman Mr. Cowan referred to—is at the door. But there is no doubt whatever that the little domestic breakages have been very numerous, and the tremendous crash when the Education Bill fell last Session nearly caused several changes in the service in John Bull's house.

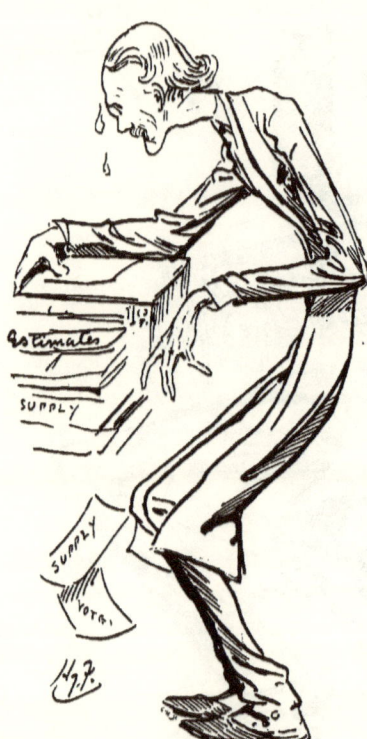

ESTIMATES

SUPPLY

SUPPLY

VOTE

EFFECT OF PUBLIC BUSINESS UPON MR. BALFOUR.

All through the Session the reputation of Mr. Joseph Chamberlain has increased in the exact proportion of the declining popularity of Mr. Balfour. No one ever undertook the Leadership of the House of Commons with better wishes from all sides than did Mr. Balfour, but his best friends must confess that he has hardly proved strong enough for the position. The question is asked, Does he work hard enough? Does he not, perhaps, trust too much to picking up the threads of serious debate on the spur of the moment, and, with his unusual cleverness, give a reply thinking on his feet? For he is more absent from the House than any other Leader, even Mr. Gladstone himself, when in his important position.

Mr. W. H. Smith, always showing the greatest attention to business, lived and almost died on the bench, and Sir William Harcourt, when acting as Leader for Lord Rosebery, was ever at his post.

At the opening of the Session, three matters deeply interested the House: Mr. Chamberlain's attitude towards the South African Chartered Company, the new Leadership of the Irish Party, and the introduction of Mr. Lecky to the House of Commons.

When Mr. Chamberlain walked into the House on February 11, he was received

IRISH LEADERS PRESENT AND PAST.

MR. DILLON.

MR. CHAPLIN CHIRPY.

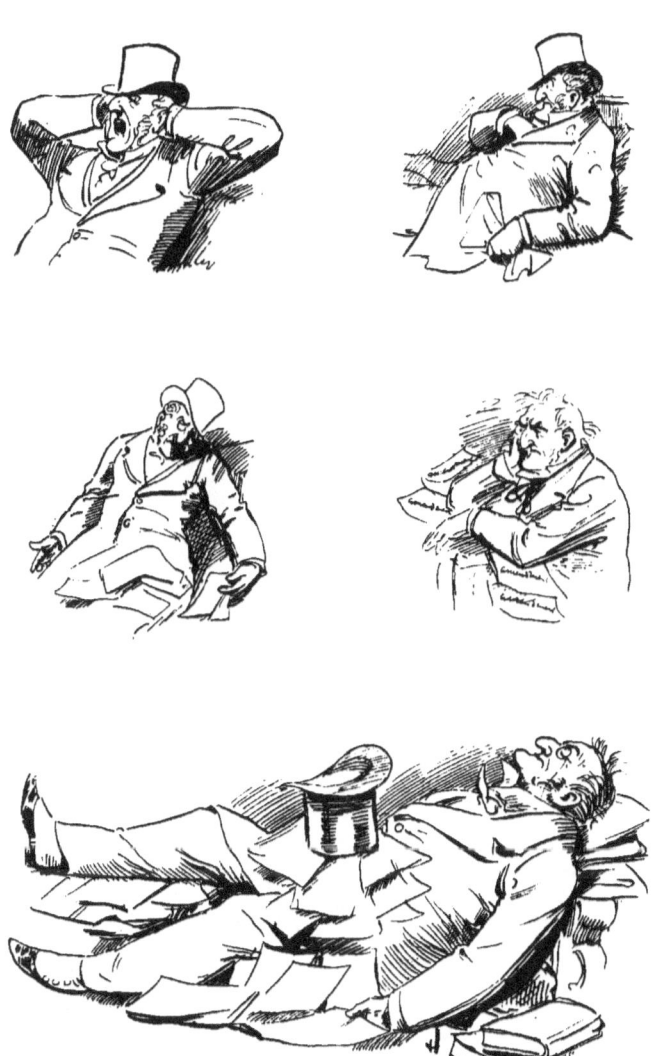

MR. CHAPLIN COLLAPSED.

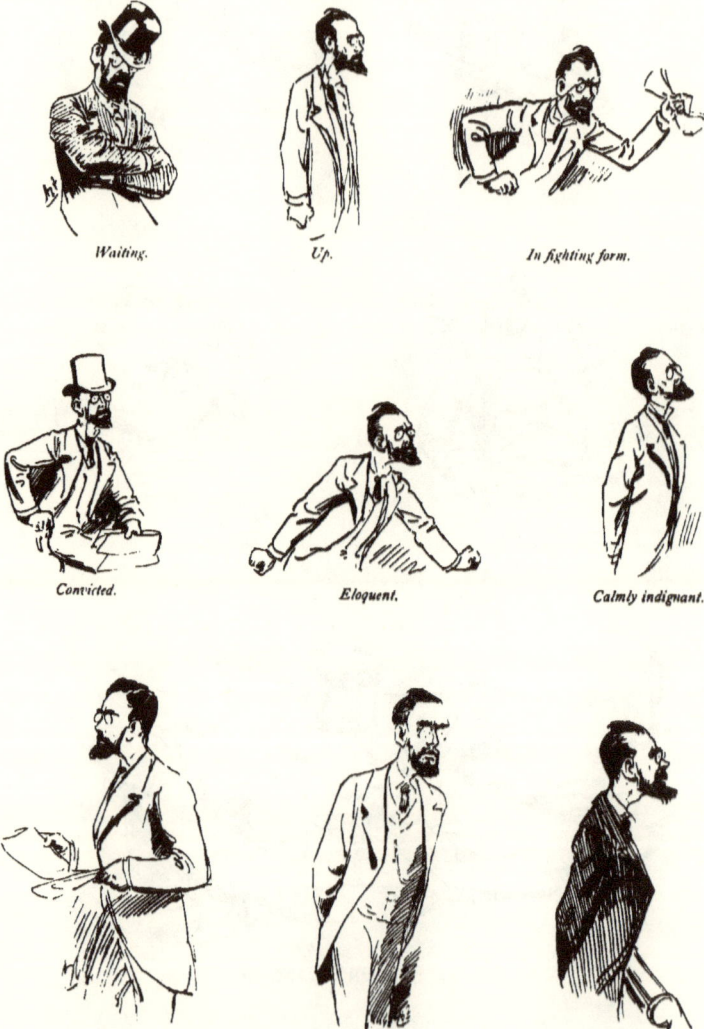

STUDIES OF 'TIM.'

'Old friends.'   *Mr. Bowles rebuking Mr. Hanbury.*

STUDIES OF 'TOMMY.'

with tremendous cheering from his supporters. But he did not rise for a day or two, and had to wait for the antics of the proprietor of 'Truth' before making his speech, which every one was looking forward to with great anxiety. The new Leader of the

A 'RASCH' ACT.

Early in the Session Major Rasch asked leave to introduce a Bill to shorten the duration of speeches, which was carried by one hundred votes.

Irish Party, Mr. Dillon, found himself thrown in the shade, not only through the cleverness of Mr. Timothy Healy, but by the more statesmanlike attitude of Mr. John Redmond ; and Mr. Lecky nearly spoilt the effect of his appearance by neglecting to complete the signing of the Roll of Parliament, and was brought back to the table to finish the specimen of penmanship which every new Member is obliged to deliver to the official of the House, on taking the oath.

Even Mr. Labouchere discovered that he could not appear in the limelight at the opening of the political pantomime, as he wished. He intended coming up a trap-door in red fire, and moving an amendment to the Address challenging the conduct and position of the Chartered Company ; but, by the rules of the House, if he did this, further debates on the subject would be precluded. He therefore had to rise at the most awkward part of the evening, when the House was empty, to make his attack upon Mr. Chamberlain and the Chartered Company ; and it was not until Mr. Chamberlain rose later in the evening that the House cared to show any interest in the matter.

Mr. Chamberlain's speech was worthy of a great occasion. He had introduced into the whole of the South African question a novelty which was refreshing ; he had thrown red-tapeism to the winds, and had communicated direct with the Press when any matter of importance had come to his hands concerning South African affairs. He had been so clear and business-like throughout the whole matter that his speech seemed to be the recital of a triumph rather than an appeal for sympathy, as most speeches made on such questions are, when given in the House. Mr. Chamberlain is a lucky man, and his luck did not desert him on this occasion. While he was unravelling the circumstances of the case, and reading the telegrams he had received from South Africa and immediately forwarded to the Press, who would have thought that, at that moment, a message would be received from President Krüger, and that message one to enhance the dramatic interest of Mr. Chamberlain's oration, and one that Mr. Chamberlain used to great effect, as he brought his speech to a close amid cheers just when the clock was striking the hour which ushered in St. Valentine ?

Mr. Dillon is a wearisome Parliamentarian, as dull as Mr. Healy is amusing and entertaining. Mr. Dillon speaks too often and too long—he believes in quantity, if not in quality—with a weak voice of whining character, and a style of delivery that never carries conviction.

The Brothers Balfour sit with their arms and legs crossed and their chins in the air, suffering the infliction without showing much interest. It is not so when Mr. Healy or Mr. Redmond, or others on the Irish benches, speak ; but Mr. Dillon has a soothing effect, if one is to judge by the closed eyelids of the Brothers Balfour.

Of course we have the Colonel Saunderson to the front again. He gave his first

THE BROTHERS BALFOUR.   LEFT IN CHARGE.

THE GOVERNMENT HERON AND THE PRIVATE MEMBER.

THE IRISH QUESTION: ATTITUDE OF THE BROTHERS BALFOUR.

MR. GOSCHEN, FIRST MONTH.

entertainment on January 12, in which perhaps the most amusing point was the remark, 'The Irish are an extraordinary prolific race. The only thing in nature which comes near to them is the Australian rabbit.' The gallant Colonel was pointing out that, if the Irish race continue to increase at the present rate, there will soon be no room on the earth' for any other nationality than descendants from the Emerald Isle.

One of those little niceties which either show the dignity or the absurdity of our Houses of Parliament—I don't know which—happened when the Speaker read the Queen's Speech from the chair. Every Member uncovered, but, strange to say, Sir Henry Campbell-Bannerman remained seated with his hat on. He explained afterwards that, probably, he was the only one who really understood the rules of the House in this matter, that Members only uncovered to hear a direct message from the Queen, but didn't uncover when the message is cooked up a second time from the Chair. Really! one would think that sensible men of the world would avoid drawing attention to the absurdities of Parliamentary etiquette, by doing what others do in cases such as this, whether correct or not.

As the cackling of geese saved Rome, so it is not more historically absurd that the cackling of Mr. Swift McNeill saved Mr. Lecky. This learned historian was fast sleeping and sinking his chances in Parliament among the silent Members, when, as the soldiers were aroused by the unusual sounds emitted by the geese, Mr. Lecky was awaked by similar strains from the classic mouth of Mr. Swift McNeill. Mr. Lecky, dubbing himself a 'young Member,' assured the House that he had no intention of speaking, but

SECOND MONTH.   THIRD MONTH.

that he could not allow Mr. McNeill's remarks to go unanswered. Mr. Lecky rose to his feet, but did not rise to the occasion. He delighted the House with his lady-like manner, and gave a further illustration that Professors in Parliament are either out of place, or not a success.

The House was accustomed last Session to the little bickerings and personal attacks, under the cover of independence, shown by those Members disappointed at not getting office. Mr. James Lowther, one of the most popular men in the House, one regrets to say, is the leader of the discontent. Of course, no one pays any attention to 'Tommy' Bowles; when he keeps within bounds, he is amusing, and it must be

QUESTION TIME.

MR. CURZON.   CHANCELLOR OF THE EXCHEQUER.
                              Past.   *Present.*

admitted that he often says something sharp and clever, but, during this last Session, he has shown himself, in his endeavour to keep up his reputation for being the *farceur* of the House, to overstep the line of good taste, for which he has been severely rebuked. Still, at times, he is amusing, and his epigrams show his journalistic training. For instance, when he was challenged by Sir Ughtred Kay-Shuttleworth for inaccuracy, he replied, 'I have approached the verge of, if I have not actually touched, inaccuracy.' And when he referred to Sir Ughtred as ' one of ascertained importance,' and the House laughed at him for his impudence, he replied with ready wit, 'Yes, he compared himself to me.' He was also very hard upon his old friend Mr. Hanbury, who sat

MR. FOWLER.

MR. DAVITT.

INDIA.
The Secretary of State at the Table.

MR. FIELD

AFRICA.

MR. LEONARD COURTNEY.

SIR E. ASHMEAD-BARTLETT GETTING IT HOT.

TURKEY.

THE PREMIER.

THE ELOQUENT DUKE.

MR. JOHN REDMOND.

THE LAND BILL SENT BACK FROM THE LORDS.

directly behind. In fact, Mr. Bowles is not a very young man in a hurry, but a gentleman, although a young man in Parliament, old in journalistic playfulness, with which he is doing his best to copy Lord Randolph Churchill. Mr. Bowles might have been thought more of, had not Lord Randolph done the same things in Parliament so well before.

Now the sympathy of every one must be with Sir John Gorst, who had the unfortunate Education Bill to pilot through the House. It is generally supposed that this gigantic mistake of the Government in introducing a tremendous Bill on the vexed question of education was one of oversight on the part of Lord Salisbury and Mr. Balfour. Lord Salisbury had promised to do something for the Bishops, and, in a casual way, had designed that Gorst should pull it through the House of Commons. Poor Sir John Gorst would have had enough in facing the insult of Sir William Harcourt alone, but he soon found he had opposition not only in front of him but to the right of him, to the left of him, and behind him. The Unionists of the Bartley order revolted; in fact, poor Sir John Gorst, who is really a very able politician without ever having a chance to show it, had years taken off his political life by this tremendous white elephant of the Government—the Education Bill.

The Landlords Relief Bill, as it was called by the Radicals, was another measure introduced in the Session, that led to sorry waste of time and to a waste of another excellent Minister, Mr. Chaplin. Mr. Chaplin has always been a fighting politician, but he had more than enough of it in driving this Bill through Parliament, the effects of which upon him I leave my pencil to describe.

Then, we had the new Navy Scheme, with Mr. Goschen at the wheel. He had a more popular subject, but still had to encounter stormy nights to guide his bark over the troubled waters of Parliament.

Mr. Gerald Balfour was also burdened with a tremendous work, and he, like Sir John Gorst and Mr. Chaplin, suffered through the overloading of the business of the House with elephantine measures, the harassing details of which are too much for the pen—the less sympathetic pencil must show the effect on the Chief Secretary for Ireland. And all this incomprehensible overburdening of the Government, called work, has, of course, told on the office and fortune of his brother, the leader of the House.

In looking over my sketches in Parliament during the Session, I frequently come across notes of the Chancellor of the Exchequer—I mean, of course, artistic notes, which show him always self-contained and always at his ease amidst the continual attacks on the great greedy Government—a Government that had provided itself with too large a parliamentary meal even to bolt, let alone to masticate and properly digest during the Session.

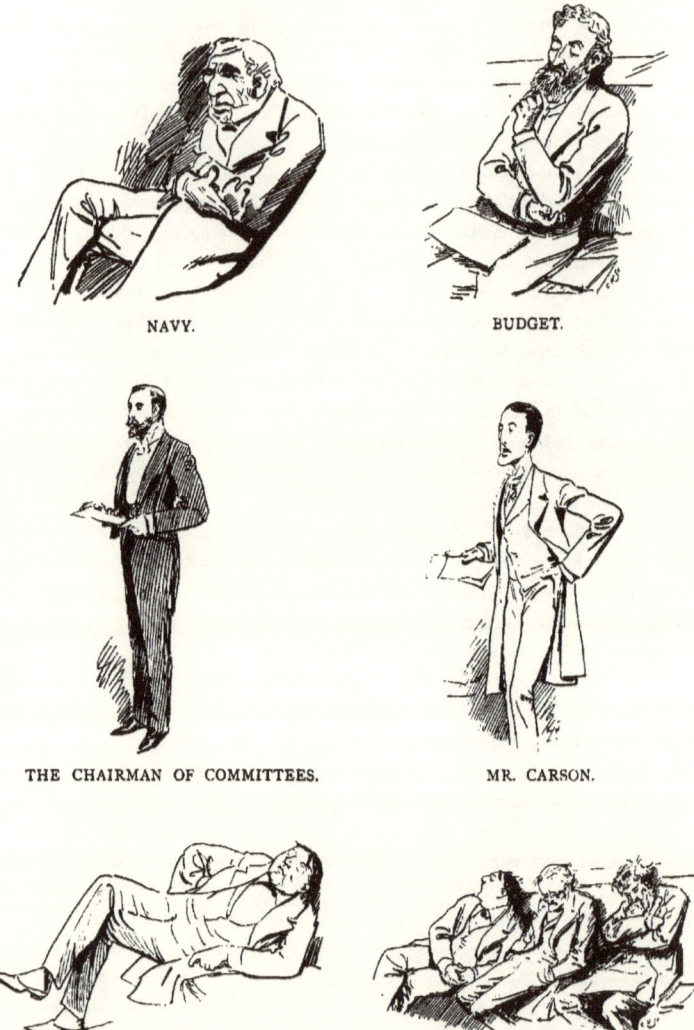

NAVY.

BUDGET.

THE CHAIRMAN OF COMMITTEES.

MR. CARSON.

'JUST LIKE BALFOUR' (MR. HANBURY).

THE GOVERNMENT BENCH.

A FEW ROUGH NOTES FROM THE PRESS GALLERY.

I find depicted in my sketches Mr. George Curzon, equally cool and collected, who is an up-to-date smart young man, and is a little too clever for Mr. Labouchere and other hecklers during question time.

Of course the Session brought its bores, a mixture of Welsh and Irish—a London-Irishman being the worst—that irrepressible Mr. Lough. Major Rasch brought in a Bill to shorten the duration of speeches, that would have snuffed out Lough and Duff and Puff and Muff, and the rest of them. Somehow, we heard nothing more about that excellent Bill, which we all agree is wanted so badly. Sir E. Ashmead-Bartlett had Egypt on the brain all the Session, and, although he was severely scolded by the two C's—Chamberlain and Curzon—like others left out in the cold, he managed to make it hot for his more fortunate friends in office.

Then we had our humorists of the Session, the most refreshing of all being our old friend Mr. Timothy Healy, who revelled in the Land Bill, and was always a relief in the rather dull debate. A fresher, perhaps, but not so finished, a humorist, was Mr. Healy's countryman, with a Paderewski appearance, Mr. Field, of Dublin. One day I recollect this gentleman's making a speech, in which two sentences are worth recording ; one was that 'The population of Ireland, which used to be 2,000,000, has, under British rule, been decimated to the extent of two-thirds'; the other, which was tragically flung across the House, that 'The time has come, and is rapidly arriving.' Mr. Labouchere may be placed between the bores and humorists—well, what is Mr. Labouchere ? But the bore *facile princeps* of the Session was, without doubt, Mr. Caldwell.

Lord Salisbury had an easier time of it in the House of Lords, which did not rise during the Session to a full-dress debate, until it came to the discussion of the Deceased Wife's Sister Bill in July. It was then that the Duke of Argyll (God bless him!) made a wonderfully fine oration ; and the present Liberal Leader in the Lords, Lord Kimberley, made a speech in strong contrast.

Perhaps, however, the most sensational event of the Session was the landlords' revolt on the Bill affecting the land in Ireland ; and they sent the Bill back to Mr. Gerald Balfour, disfigured beyond recognition with amendments. Mr. Curzon held the landlords' brief in the Commons, and consultations frequently took place in the Lobby during the Session.

But stranger things have happened since last Session. Of those I have nothing to say. My few Parliamentary jottings finished in the autumn, when I went to study our American cousins in their Congress, and to see what Parliament was like in Ottawa ; and, by the time this little book appears, I shall be on my way to study the Australian Legislators at work.

WIND UP OF A SESSION.

THE Parliamentary orchestra which the Speaker conducts has wound up its music of the Session, and the Speaker, deserted by all, strongly resembles the conductor in Haydn's celebrated Farewell Symphony. Everyone is familiar with the origin of that piece. The facts I cannot be sure of, for I am writing this far away from books of reference, and I do not pretend to have extensive knowledge of musical history. Once upon a time (that is always a safe way to begin) a certain King—the King of Saxony, I believe—found that he had to cut down his expenditure. Luxury is the first item to be crossed off by anyone in so unfortunate a position, and this extravagant ruler's particular weakness being for orchestral music, he gave notice to quit to his fiddlers three, and the other members of his famous band. Haydn came to the rescue with a farewell symphony, and endowed his musical effort with an artistic—a theatrically artistic—effect. The band begins the piece with a full orchestra. One by one its members cease playing, fold up their music, place each instrument jn its case or box, drop a tear, and sadly, but silently, take leave of the platform. The air is kept up until one alone remains—he plays the last notes, and departs. The conductor still beats time, eventually looks up, surprised to find himself alone, bows to Royalty, and retires.

I doubt whether the Members of the Parliamentary band drop a tear when they depart for their holidays from St. Stephen's, or that their conductor—the Speaker— remains long in the chair after the last M.P. quits the House; and I may question whether he looks sad when he finds they have departed, or will be glad when they are unexpectedly called back to their places. Haydn had it all his own way; his men played in harmony by doing exactly what they ought to do. They were picked men, and made themselves heard only when they were wanted, and always obeyed every wish of their conductor. How different it is with the Speaker of the House of Commons! He cannot select his players, and they will not follow his beat. The result is discord. When they return, the same old musicians will take their places, the same old tunes will be played, the frightful discord repeated. The chief difficulty with the band is that certain Members insist on blowing their own trumpets, and ruining the harmony of the House. In fact, the wind instruments have it all their own way. The first violin is the most genial of men, and one whose only wish is to do his duty to his orchestra and conductor; but the big drum will make itself heard. Has it not 'Historicus' written upon one side, and Sir William on the other? The Irish harp has an American metallic sound about it, and the Scotch bagpipes never cease in bursting forth with a frightfully unmusical sound, I cannot describe. The Welsh harp also has lost its modern value, and the brass of the English Members is unbearable. Now that the Session is over, Members of the Parliamentary band travel in the country, some perhaps in scratch bands of three or four Members, others playing singly for the edification of their not too exacting constituents. Metaphorically speaking, men who are not fit to play upon a comb or a penny whistle, attempt in their own circles solos on the most difficult instruments.

One must have 'an ear for music' fully to appreciate the difference between music and noise; and, strange as it may seem, one must really credit the fact—that it is equally necessary to have a correct ear for politics, so as to detect the value of the serious politician, compared with the blatant, bawling balderdash of the tricky and cheeky obstructionist. When I meet the conductor (I should say the Speaker) of the House · taking his constitutional not a hundred miles from Westminster, looking sad and jaded, I often wonder what he thinks of the perpetual pibroch, the rasping harps, or the discordant brass. However, he has made his bow, for the last Member has departed, and he is 'off,' either to flourish the golf club instead of the bâton, if he is bitten with the latest craze, or, perhaps, to call the grouse to order, or name the sluggish fish. What a relief it will be for the courteous Serjeant-at-Arms to remove the mace from the

SCENES IN THE HOUSE OF COMMONS: AT THE END OF THE SESSION.

table, and fly to his native heather, and shoulder a gun instead! The leader of the House gave his last smile of the Session days ago, and departed, with the first violin in its case, and the best of wishes from all sides went with him. Mr. Labouchere has walked across the road with the skull-cap on his head—to fetch his 'Parliamentary hat,' left on the seat of the Parliamentary orchestra. The House is an admirable place for him to try over his latest composition. The manuscript is published—considerably cut down—in his paper. His favourite piece has not yet been played with the success he hopes for; it is 'Labouchere's Farewell Symphony to the House of Lords.'

The Ladies' Gallery is nearly empty, but one or two remain to hear the last note. The Speaker's Secretary stands patiently under the gallery, to see the last Member depart, and to support the conductor for the last time in his official duties. The Speaker's Secretary has much to do, and all appreciate his tact and labour when the piece of the day has to be prepared. He has all his work in going over the various compositions and scoring them, so as to bring them into harmony in the best way possible.

Chief-Inspector Horsley is left in charge. His name suggests that, like another well-known gentleman of his name, he objects to anything disrobed, and a naked House of Commons is a poor thing to watch over. Perhaps the popular 'man in possession' would not object to find the band recalled immediately, as they were in the Farewell Symphony of the great composer. But they may come and beat the drum and blow the trombone, and make the fiddles squeak, the bagpipes screech, and the harps whine. I repeat, my ear is not a musical one, and my political ears are still ringing with fourteen years of these most discordant voices.

www.ingramcontent.com/pod-product-compliance
Lightning Source LLC
Chambersburg PA
CBHW030537040726
47497CB00008B/2488